Burn Bright

Burn Bright

Nancy Hall

Library of Congress Cataloging-in-Publication Data

ISBN: 979-8-9888614-3-0

Printed and bound in the United States of America by Ingram Lightning Source

First edition

Cover design: Wanda Stanfill

Editing, layout, and design: Jacque Hillman and Katie Gould

The HillHelen Group LLC
470 North Parkway, Suite C
Jackson, TN 38305

The HillHelen Group LLC
635 North 65th Place
Mesa, AZ 85205

(731) 394-2894
www.hillhelengrouppublishers.com
hillhelengroup@gmail.com

For Jacque
An extraordinary woman,
editor, and friend

Acknowledgments

My gratitude to these for all your effort and support:

The HillHelen Group makes this book possible. Thank you, Jacque and Katie, for your constant, detailed good work. Wanda Stanfill, the cover and artwork is perfect.

To those writers who share their work and encouragement at writing retreats and online classes, you inspire me.

My hometown, which is the seedbed of my creative energies.

My yoga practice.

Of course to all the dogs in my life. Those I have known and those I have heard about. All you four-legged, cold-nosed tail waggers—here's a pat on the head.

Contents

PART I
THE SETUP

Edna's Secrets

Two things are constant in my life. The moon and meanness. Both have their time to shine or hide in the darkness and wait.

I wrestle with meanness most every day. Like old dead George. Some days, it's on me. Other days, it's a reckoning that pops up. But the moon keeps me steady.

Hesitation spells doom. I nearly waited too long this time. I thought Edna Love knew everything about living and dying.

Secrets entice us. They exist everywhere. Some hang over us. Some we bury. Some are paybacks doled out piece by piece. But secrets work on us all.

I carried a secret that lightened as each year passed. But I still hid the secret that made me who I am today. Gave me resolve and courage but stole my sleep some nights. We all have secrets. God knows Edna Love's got a whole pocketful.

One night after I had been in Nuanz for nearly a year, I confessed my horrible, soul-worthy secret to Edna Love. I had killed old George. He deserved to die for raping me. I left his evil sunk in a Mississippi swamp.

She told me about her own day of reckoning—a guy named Freddie. I remember she took those glittery chopsticks out of her hair, tapped them against her open palm, and said, "See these—one is for good and one is for evil. You gotta keep both of them within your sight—hold 'em close. Goodness is not always the path to take. Revenge gets you there, too."

I never knew for sure if her love story survival was due to the good one or the evil one. She kept those chopsticks positioned just so in her upswept bouffant hairdo. They were always there, guiding her through this world of ours. I sure as hell was willing to listen and even follow if needed.

The first Christmas I lived in Nuanz, I gave Edna Love a little black book inscribed *Edna's Secrets*. When I gave it to her, she laughed so hard I thought she was gonna keel over right there.

"Law, honey, I can't write all of that down."

But, I swear, the more I learn about Edna, I fear there's not enough little black books in the world to hold her secrets. I want to discover as many as I can. Edna has most everything figured out. At least I thought that until this past spring.

Secrets can paralyze you, too. They can put you in a grave you dig yourself long before you're dead. Every secret wants to be told. Some people catch on fire when they learn somebody's got a secret. I guess it's human nature. Edna Love is one of the most open women I have ever known, but she has a whole book full of secrets.

Some deal with petty things. Spats between kinfolk or threats made but not carried out. It's all about how you look at it. That depends on how you've lived your life so far.

Edna's secrets may involve no-account lowlifes and haughty, fame-seeking scoundrels. These are the ones worth something. Not necessarily money—but leverage. Leverage and blackmail are close companions. She guards those and wields power because you never quite know how Edna is going to react. This was a side Edna honed over the years. I needed to take some lessons from her.

Edna walked the edge in her tottery high heels with her Clairol Midnight Black French twist, but she had never fallen over until that spring. I didn't recognize her fall from the edge at first. When I did finally figure it out, it was almost too late. Those secrets were coming back to haunt us here in Nuanz.

2

Same Old Shenanigans

We were at our usual places in the Bluebird Cafe in Nuanz on a Monday morning. I was delivering plates of eggs, sausage, toast, and grits loaded in butter. Mr. Rob was plopping the plates on the serve-through window shelf as fast as he could. He pushed his worn, soda-jerk white hat to the back of his head. The two bluebirds had faded on both sides. Or maybe that was an extra layer of grease.

The bluebird logo flies across the front of our cafe aprons. Thank goodness there are plenty of pockets, but I usually stick my pencil over my left ear if I am busy. Sometimes I do a double take when I catch my reflection in the window. Who is that young woman with a smile on her face? I thought I was always serious.

Waitresses come and go here, except me. Mr. Rob supplies each full-time waitress with two dress uniforms. Otherwise, we are on our own with skirts, blouses, and slacks. Our aprons hang on the back wall. Sometimes I pick up an odd apron, and it hangs below my knees.

Today, I was in a long one. I don't mind wrapping the sash in the back and tying it in the front as long as it doesn't get in my way.

Edna stopped by to start her day. I stood behind the counter during the lull of the midmorning coffee break. She stared into her cup and sighed.

Here we go again, I thought. I knew Edna had been down in the dumps. She goes through this spell every so often. She complained many times that she would be better off down in sunny Florida than here in sad, old Nuanz. But this year seemed worse. Something was gnawing at her, and I couldn't find out what it was. Her voice didn't have that lilt to it. She sparkled but not as brightly.

She frowned at me. "Mesha, I am just so tired of all of this."

I stayed still. "All of what?"

"You know. People want something all the time. Same old complaints. Same old shenanigans. The gossips always hunting more gossip."

Pot calling kettle, I thought, knowing Edna stored gossip like gold. I grabbed a wet rag to mop down the counter. "That's the way of the world, isn't it? Can't really change some things, you know."

"I know. But I . . ." She drifted away as she studied her folded hands on the countertop. "I want more. I just wish I could be in love one more time before I die."

She spoke so softly I had to lean over to hear the last word.

"But, Edna, you are loved."

"No, hon. Being loved and being in love are two different things." She lifted her eyes to my face, and behind those eyes was a sadness I had never noticed before.

"Maybe I am too old, and my chances are gone. But I remember how it feels. I want to feel that way again. Is that so bad?" She propped her elbows on the counter and rested her chin on her hands.

I turned the rag over and went over the same small space I had been scrubbing.

"No. I don't think it's bad. Kind of human nature, isn't it? You just gotta work at it maybe." Who was I to be telling Edna Love anything about life?

She drummed her fingers on the counter. "Like that sash in the front, sugar. I should be mad 'cause you can wrap it so many times around your waist. It's not fair." She smiled a little.

"You missed a spot." Her fire-engine red nails scratched at a dried patch of egg on the counter.

"Thanks."

I pushed the wet rag in tiny, whiplike turns across the lunch counter.

The door opened, and two old maids—Miss Medlock and her longtime friend Miss Lewis—wandered back to their usual table. Edna raised her left eyebrow at me. "See? Two queens of the Lonely Hearts Club," she mumbled, lowering her voice.

"But you know what I mean about being in love. Like those goosebumps that crawl on the back of your head when you see him. Or you forget to eat and get lightheaded."

I gazed at Edna Love.

"No, I don't know what you mean. I probably never will."

The countertop glistened now. I picked up the sugar canister and gave it a good wipe. Then I glanced at my personal idol again.

"What's that you say all the time? Can't anybody save you but yourself?"

She shook her head. "That has nothing to do with this, Mesha. It's just . . . I don't know."

"You get this way every once in a while because nothing's going on. Remember last year when you was threatening to sell out and move to Clearwater and ride on those glass-bottomed boats? Or to Key West and open a really fine Oasis Club there?"

She grabbed her purse from the stool and stood up. Ordinarily, she would have winked or patted my hand, then waved at the men in the back. She counted out some change on the counter.

I turned to check on Mr. Thornton's ham sandwich. Edna started toward the door, and I thought I heard her say goodbye. The bell over the door dinged. Her coffee cup was still full.

After most of the lunch crowd left, I saw Henry, the brown spotted pointer, sitting by the front door peeking in. He knew it was either bacon or biscuit-and-gravy time. Henry and me had become friends.

Everybody knew Henry. He was probably the smartest dog any of us had ever known. He had to be, living with the Malones, who had a bunch of stair-stepped kids in the family. Their house was the one where the neighborhood kids gathered.

Mrs. Malone was an easygoing woman from Mississippi. She was full of grace and tended to let her children figure out life's lessons on their own, unless they really needed a little guidance. Mr. Malone's family went back several generations in Dayton County. There was always room for one more at their table loaded with food. There were usually enough young bodies for backyard football or keep-away or Indian torture tricks.

The oldest Malone son and his buddies took Henry hunting when they were still too young to drive. Henry would lead them down a dusty road into Taylor's Woods until he found a nice covey. The boys followed on their bikes, and Henry waited for them at the edge of the field.

His nose and sense of direction were not the only remarkable thing about this dog. I learned that one day while I was sitting on the front steps waiting for the last customer to leave the cafe. Mr. Gordon joined me, and we both turned as Henry strolled up the hill from Rem's Place. Mr. Gordon stood there with his arms folded and said, "That's Henry Malone. The smartest dog you'll ever see."

Of course, I asked why he was the smartest dog ever.

"Well, a few years ago, Dr. Hunt, the vet over there on Huntingdon Street, heard a scratching on the door and found Henry sitting there. He didn't see any of the Malones and thought they must have dropped him off. Doc invited him in and put him on his exam table. It wasn't time for any shots. He didn't have any nicks or ticks. But the dog kept looking at him and waiting. Doc gave him a B-12 shot, you know, to ease his arthritis up a bit, and then waited for the Malones to come back. Near closing time, he walked out the door, and Henry jumped down and took off toward home. Doc called Lawyer Malone later and said, 'I gave Henry his shot. Guess he made it home okay?'"

Mr. Gordon leaned in to be sure I was paying attention. "Guess what?

The Malones hadn't brought him. He came down on his own. Still does every so often when his arthritis gets to acting up."

He shook his head and grinned. "Now how's that for a smart dog?"

So I figured I was a smart person to be friends with a smart dog who knew everything. I snuck him treats, and before long, I knew he preferred bacon or biscuits—with gravy, of course. He knew our specials at the Bluebird, I am not kidding. Maybe he could smell the bacon grease. I don't know. But he showed up on his favorite meal days.

Sometimes I'd sit on the bench outside and talk to Henry. He listened like he understood me. I liked having another friend who was easy come, easy go, but looked at me so intently with his big brown eyes.

Days got busy at the Bluebird. Henry kept to his meal schedule. Some days, I whispered my secrets into his ears.

I didn't think about Edna and her wishes again until Sheriff Willard Hensley came by a few days later during the lunch rush. He stood at the counter until I had a minute to breathe.

He asked me when I had last seen Edna. That's unusual because the sheriff and Edna are close, you know. A tall, muscled man with sandy hair and blue eyes, he held his khaki sheriff's cap in his hands and quizzed me, gently, though. He and his wife have been kind to me. Once he looks over his glasses like he does, his blue eyes aren't soft; they look into your heart and know stuff.

"What do you mean?" I asked.

"She hasn't been seen around town for a while."

"So sometimes she takes off."

I watched the fresh coffeepot fill. I needed to work the men's table in the back. The sheriff didn't take the hint.

"That crippled man that works at Love's Launderette brought three bags of coins to the Bank of Nuanz this morning. Says Edna hasn't been by to pick up the deposit."

"Well, maybe he forgot that she was going somewhere."

I picked up the full coffeepot to make my rounds. The sheriff peered over his glasses at me.

"Are you sure she didn't mention leaving town?"

"Not that I remember. But I am not her mother, you know. She makes a run to Memphis occasionally. Maybe she found something to get into."

The sheriff shrugged his shoulders and followed me to speak to the men. I didn't give it another thought. Court was in session on a Thursday, and we were busy. Lots of people besides our usual crowd waited to be fed. Something nagged at me, but I didn't have time to pursue it.

At the close of the day, I stood outside the Bluebird Cafe and, still in my apron, leaned against the front plate-glass window. Lawyer Malone locked his office across the street and lifted his hand good night to me. Just as the quietness settled in, there was a sudden burst of laughter, and a few notes from the jukebox at Pierce's Pool Room drifted over. The last rays of the setting sun struck the west side of the courthouse clock tower, and the pigeons circled but didn't land. I went back inside to close, said good night to Lolly, and checked the locker for the breakfast supplies. Tomorrow was delivery day.

My upstairs apartment in the Friedman Building next door was forty-two steps away. I gathered my last spurt of energy and climbed the stairs. Setting my leftovers on the counter, I sprawled across the bed with my book. But I couldn't concentrate in the quiet. No voices, no bells ringing, no shouts of "order up," no motors humming. Just my thoughts bouncing off the walls. *Meshac Brownlow, what's going on in your feeble brain?*

Moon dark began this week. The shadows grew in from the edges of this darkest moon phase between midnight and three in the morning when the nocturnal cycle began. Under this perfect blanket of darkness, I woke up suddenly. Had I heard something? I staggered to my bedroom window to look out over the square.

I craned my head and felt the cool glass against my cheek. As I peered through my window, my breath fogged the pane. The court-square lights went off at midnight, so some starlight made its way through the trees in downtown Nuanz.

As I stood and watched, two men crossed the square heading toward Paradise Alley. One was tall and skinny; the other was big with a mass of hair. They didn't look familiar to me, but there were still lots of folks in Nuanz I had never run across. But their solitary journey made me think of other nighttime travelers, one of whom I had been not too long ago.

3

Prior Lives

I moved downtown next door to the Bluebird Cafe last summer. There was an apartment in the Friedman Building over the Tom C. Harbert Insurance Agency. Mr. Harbert, who owned the agency, was also the man to see to rent any space. Known as Little Tom, he was a friendly man you could trust and one of my regular customers.

When the apartment became vacant, he asked me if I was interested. I jumped at the chance to be in town, where I felt safer, because moving ended my solitary walks from the Nuanz Motor Inn. The apartment on the square was quieter than at the motel, where I lived for the first few years in Nuanz. Out there was more traffic. Doors slammed at all hours of the night. Car lights from the highway washed over the building.

Once I knew I could manage the rent, I didn't hesitate. I didn't own a car, and walking to the Bluebird Cafe for my morning shifts was never quite the same after my kidnapping a few years ago. I was always vigilant even when I told myself I wasn't scared.

But I liked being upstairs at the Friedman Building and such a short distance from the cafe. There were others who lived downtown, too. Mr. and Mrs. Hays lived over their grocery store on the square's south side. They were older, but it was nice knowing someone was nearby if I needed to scream for help. An attorney, Mr. Harwood, often slept at his law office a few doors down since his wife died. His office was the first in Lawyers Row on the west side of the square.

Nuanz, Tennessee, was a typical small town. The county seat boasted a mighty fine courthouse and, during the day, a downtown that held most anything you might need. After hours, the beer joints and taverns came alive and were scattered a block or two off the square. Rem's for the black folks was a block north. Edna Love's Oasis was three blocks west. Pierce's Pool Room on the lower east side was usually dark by eleven o'clock. Other joints came and went, but most stayed off the square. It felt safe. I could have privacy but be in the midst of others, too, if I needed them.

I felt older and more settled in the apartment. Edna, my closest friend and arbitrary mother, donated a bed and a rocker. I was able to buy a few things at a time until now it felt like a home. The apartment had a sitting room, tiny kitchen, bedroom, and bath.

Best of all, there were two windows that overlooked the court square. I could see not only the historic Dayton County Courthouse, but also here on the west side was the fancy water fountain with a few goldfish and the David Crockett statue with his face turned looking east. Meanwhile, the Confederate soldier statue loomed up nearly as high as the oak trees on the east side. There was also a grave on the northwest side that I could barely make out from my window. Having bones buried there was kind of weird. Death is never too far away.

The sun rose over the Knox Feed Store, Wade Dry Cleaners, and Huckaby Drug Store on the east side of the square each day. At night, the moon and first stars would make their appearance there before moving to the west.

When I moved into my apartment in the Friedman Building, I was so taken with the court square and the majestic courthouse that I spent a lot of time gazing out my window. Downtown held most of the business section of the town. There were banks, law offices, insurance agencies, a feed store, two drugstores, a couple of department stores, and one doctor.

The local optometrist, Dr. Huffman, had a corner office in my building on the second floor across from me. He was a quiet, slow-talking man who worked alone. He kept a steady stream of patients, from old farmers with rheumy eyes to cross-eyed kids. His front desk stayed piled up with papers and folders. The blue haze of cigarette smoke wandered over the landing as he forgot to open his windows.

The Selective Service Board had a front office next to me with two small rooms and a cranky older woman to answer the phone and open the mail. On the other side of Dr. Huffman was a young lawyer just opening his practice. Most everyone left by six at the latest unless the lawyer had a hot court case he was cramming for.

I always had the place to myself at night. There was a back entrance to the second floor from the alley. A flight of stairs led to the door that opened onto the landing. The lawyer and his clients mainly used this door. Beyond the stairs was an outside fire escape that led onto the roof. The first time I tried it out, I was a little shaky. That first rung was a stretch. This building wasn't the tallest building downtown but was the same height as the others in the block. There was a half wall marking off the buildings, and the roof was a couple of feet below it. The wall felt protective enough if you stood there. There were drains running down the back and over to the side alley. A couple of pipes were hooded, and in the winter, they released a bit of warmth that floated into the air. There was only a two-foot-wide wall between this building and the roof of the cafe.

The cafe had a facade facing the square that held a window and what looked like a small room behind it. There were big, rotating fans that connected to the kitchen. On the other side of the cafe was the hardware store, and a bank was on the corner. The fire escape that ran from the Friedman Building seemed to work for all three buildings. Those small, easily stepped-over pediments were the firewalls between the buildings.

But when I discovered this outside place, I saw it as a space for me to be completely alone. I could gaze at the sky, watch the moon rise, and find the north star. No one could see me. No cars passing around the square could pull over and ask me how to get to Dyersburg. I would be completely on my own. Needless to say, I climbed up on the roof frequently if the weather permitted.

Tonight, I needed a quick getaway to settle myself down. I grabbed my blanket and a thermos of tea and climbed up to watch the last of the sunset, filled with orange and pinks, and the beginning of nightfall. The sun sank slowly in the west. A few clouds had lingered, and the first star appeared before halfway dark. I leaned against the wall's warmth in my secret hiding place. It reminded me of Grace at the Nuanz Motor Inn when she would climb in the maple tree across from my room and spy on me.

A few cars and trucks moved out of town down the highway. The pigeons would be coming into the clock tower soon to roost, swooping, cooing, and pooping until the night told them to settle in. The car lights bumped over the railroad tracks and began to carve a way through the quickly settling dusk.

I poured out my last cup of tea from the thermos and felt the heat of the bricks against my stomach and arms as they dangled over the wall. I scanned the sky for the next star.

As my eyes lowered over the fields stretching out to the west, I saw a steady glow of light near the railroad trestle that crossed over the river. The glow sputtered briefly and then started again. A campfire maybe? Too early for kids to be camping out, but this was far enough away from the farmhouses and buildings. Must be some guys up to no good. There were a couple of beer joints between the jail and the motel on the highway headed north. But anyone would have had to do some hiking to get that far. More than likely, these fire starters had walked down the railroad tracks and jumped down to set the blaze.

I couldn't see any lights yet at the Oasis. Sometimes in the quiet, I could hear voices there as the patrons arrived or left. Right now, there was mostly silence, coldness, and that fire.

I turned my back and stared at the courthouse clock. All four sides of the clock displayed a different time. The west side of the clock said twenty till four. The south side said straight-up noon.

The clock's bell would chime whatever it felt like, never right since I had been here. At straight-up midnight, the clock would tell you it's just five o'clock. I love Nuanz.

When I finished my tea, I saw the moon begin to rise and located the Milky Way. If I could swallow the moonlight like an antidote to the darkness inside of me, I would do it. I would drink liquid moonlight—a thousand times I would.

I turned back west again and saw two—no, three—fires. I squeezed my eyes shut and opened them again to be sure. Why would anyone light three fires? They formed a semicircle of sorts. I couldn't figure out exactly where they were. Darkness could fool you like that. Surely if they were burning something down, somebody would know it. But it was cold, and my tea was gone, and I was ready for bed. I climbed down, locked up, and trotted to my cozy apartment.

4

Home Free?

I had big ambitions for my life now that I was living here in Nuanz. My growing-up years were spent in a piss-poor town way down in Mississippi called Wicket. It was more like Wicked. There were five children at home at one time, but when I broke free, only my alcoholic mother, younger sister Irene, and brother Roy were left.

Wicket was a lost cause for me after my daddy died and my older brothers left home. The chances of me ever doing much for myself there were slim to none. There was an underlying feeling of us versus them. It wasn't that race thing, either. We didn't mix with the blacks. Most everybody was classified according to the haves and the have-nots. Land, money, and positions.

Since I came to Nuanz, though, I had learned about people. Of course, I was only seventeen when I left home after I murdered my mother's boyfriend. He had taken me to the back seat of our family car and raped me when I was only ten years old. It took me a long time to make my move, but I was spurred by remembering my daddy and trying to protect my little sister Irene. The funny thing is that I came all the way up here but still don't feel completely safe. Yeah, Mr. Hunter helped me dump George's body in Hale's Swamp. Nobody has come after me yet, but I still feel jittery at times.

Edna Love took me in when I arrived, and Grace Robinson, who is just a kid, became my loyal protector. I tried to pay back the universe and do my penance. I kept my head down, got a job, and stayed quiet. Then Grace's little black friend Noah was murdered and thrown into the whites-only swimming pool. I saw that as my calling, my payback—find the bastard who had done that and make him pay. I did. Edd Biggs is wasting away in the state penitentiary, and I hope I never see that smarmy, little, dried-up man again.

But I know in my heart that I am not home free yet. That's why I try not to get too happy and carefree. I carry a burden that I expect to have until I die. But let me tell you that I don't regret killing George, not one bit. Old dead George deserved everything me and Fate delivered.

5

What's a Nuanz?

Nuanz is a peculiar name for a town. At first, I thought it was named after somebody. Of course, I guess it didn't seem peculiar if you lived there all your life. The crowd at the Bluebird never thought anything about their hometown's name. But I wondered.

One day, Miss Lewis, a retired schoolteacher, was writing a check for the two pies she was picking up. As she bowed her head over the checkbook, I followed her careful, precise, cursive writing. Being me, I struck up a conversation with her.

"Is this the Tuesday Bridge Club or the Thursday Canasta group?"

"It's the Nuanz Literary Club," she said, focused on her writing. She pronounced it *Noo-ahnz*, long and drawn out.

I said, "Exactly who is Mr. Nuanz? Where'd he come from?"

She gave me that schoolteacher stare. "There is no Mr. Nuanz."

"Oh, I guess it's named after Mrs. Nuanz then? Came over on the *Mayflower* or something?"

She still didn't crack a smile. "You're not from around here, are you?"

"No, ma'am, you know I come from off." That's my standard answer if someone asks where I am from.

She went over her check to be sure everything was proper, slowly tearing the paper from one side to the other in her checkbook, and handed it to me.

"Well, think about it. *Noo-ahnz*. Drop the *z* and add *c-e*."

I am a big reader, and I didn't get what she meant at first. Then she said, "Have you ever heard of *nuance*?" She spelled it for me then, slowly, as if I didn't have a lick of sense.

"*N-u-a-n-c-e*." She nodded.

I grinned. "Oh, that never popped into my head."

She smiled then. I know she probably wanted to say she knew several things that weren't in my head, but being the lady she is, she didn't.

She held up the ballpoint pen and raised her eyebrows at me. I nodded and said, "Sure, keep it. It's yours."

"No one knows exactly who named our town. Some say a young woman suggested the name to her father as a sort of joke, and he liked the sound."

Miss Lewis folded her checkbook and placed it and the Bluebird Cafe pen in her pocketbook.

"I like to think it describes us here. We all have our nuances. Very few people are who they say they are or who they pretend to be." She stood straight with her shoulders back. "Sometimes evil may be hidden, but a nuance tells us differently. Veracity is not always the norm. A nuance here and there is expected. Intriguing even."

I looked at Miss Lewis for a long moment.

"Where's my receipt?"

I put my friendly waitress face on and slapped the receipt onto the counter.

"Need any help carrying this out to the car?"

"No, I think I can manage."

She winked at me then (why I don't know), loaded up the pies, and left. Nuanz, Tennessee—quite a glorified name for a little town.

When I came to Nuanz, I felt different here. I was scared and alone, but I had met the devil and escaped. My life should have felt different. After a while, I felt like I belonged. If you belong to a place and the place belongs to you, there is a hole inside of you that only being there can fill. I can tell you that neither the place nor the people are quite enough, but it's something else that's hard to describe.

It's as if something there has seeped into your pores more than skin deep. You may notice it when someone suddenly calls your name across a grocery aisle, or a roomful of unlikely people talk quietly of ordinary things. You are a part of them without even intending to be. Even the smell of the yeasty doughnuts that lift dawn each morning and the silence that happens before nightfall—these ordinary things wrap around us and tie us to this place.

Sometimes there may be a knot of resentment still stuck somewhere inside you. That doesn't always go away. Some folks come to a place seeking revenge or forgiveness. You may hope that you can change. Maybe you can let go of the past, be comforted, or move on. If you truly belong to a place, then you only feel completely whole when you are there. Both the good and bad—all wrapped up together.

There are big differences between many of us here, but our humanness still sticks out. For instance, take the Whittakers. They were early settlers in this little town. Their last name appeared on the first lots sold. The Whittakers bought land, raised families, served in the wars, and scattered a bevy of descendants over the county. At one time, they had a fine house on Main Street full of smart children. Some married and moved to the city. Some left and never came back. A few fell into crime. All that's left now is the last remnant of who they used to be—Mr. and Mrs. Whittaker and their son, Benny.

The adults tolerate them. Some try to help. Dr. McRee treats their physical health. The county judge oversees their mental health. He had to commit Mrs. Whittaker from time to time to Western State to try and keep the peace.

Mostly, the Whittakers roam the streets and get into minor scrapes with the law. The kids are afraid of them. Mrs. Whittaker is mean and intimidating. She is tall and thin and wears a lopsided felt hat with a faded pink flower pulled low on her head. She always has a purse hanging from her bony shoulder. She mutters a lot and will swing her purse at you. Mr. Whittaker walks all bent over, wearing scuffed shoes and patched clothes. He makes a living sharpening saws and scissors. The three of them walk everywhere in a line. She leads, the old man follows behind her, and the son trails along in the gutter. All they used to have is gone—along with their minds.

The Taliafarro families were here from the beginning, too. There was a prominent, white Taliafarro family who laid out the original town and started a foundry. They prospered early and left their name on legal contracts, prime real estate, and cemetery headstones. Their name stayed with their slaves. The black Taliafarros endured while the white Taliafarros disappeared.

Today, the black Taliafarros are all that's left. They began with little but know how to hold on. Those Taliafarros acquired their own stealthy power and independence. The white people in Nuanz respect the family but don't really know their full prominence and strengths.

Both families belong to Nuanz, and both claim a place here. If called on, the people of Nuanz protects its citizens. After all, each of us is only one step away from disaster on any given day.

Here in Nuanz, we might have our share of crazies, questionable characters, or even sorry SOBs. But they belong to us. We can't help but claim them.

That is why when Guido Salvatorre came to town, we should have known there would be trouble. He unleashed something that we couldn't figure out at first. I certainly should have figured it out since I was a stranger here, too—not so long ago. We should have known.

6

Where's Edna?

The next day at the Bluebird Cafe was another day of scorched coffee, burned bacon, and sticky counters. Everybody and everything were out of sorts.

This was the time when I would usually hook up with Edna and get the skinny on everything. Then I remembered that she had disappeared for a few days. I finished sweeping under the back tables, and as I made my way back to the kitchen, there was someone standing on the sidewalk. The little crippled man from Love's Launderette was staring in the plate-glass window. He shaded his eyes and leaned against the glass to see better. Then he knocked on the glass—*bap, bap, bap*—and rattled the ladies in the front booth. I waved him in, but he motioned for me to come outside.

I stood at the open door. "What do you want, Clubby?"

"I'm looking for Miss Edna. Have you seen her?" His voice was high and whiny.

"No, did you try down at . . ."

"I tried everywhere—the Oasis, her house, the pool room . . ."

He laid his forearm across the window and hung his head. His voice shook.

I walked outside. "What's wrong?"

"I ain't seen her in a whole bunch of days, and I'm afraid somebody's gonna rrrob me."

"The sheriff said she's been gone for a few days. Maybe she . . ."

He interrupted. He wasn't listening.

"People know she's gone. I been sleeping on a bag of coins sometimes when she don't come by. Now I got four bags. I can't sleep on four bags of coins. It's asking too much." He pressed his lips together and shook his head.

"I don't know what I'm gonna do. There's a couple of machines gone out and I—I don't know if I should call Bobby Joe or not. She's gonna be mad if they close down the laundry mat. I know she will." His eyes darted around like those pigeons at the clock tower.

"Yeah, you're right there. But I don't know what to tell you."

He sniffed like he was all choked up or something. "Well, I ain't got another place to sleep except there. And, and, and, and, uh . . ."

He muttered something else I couldn't understand. Then he walked off mumbling.

"She'll show up. Hang in there," I hollered, but he kept walking, his little body balanced on the built-up shoe, weaving from side to side.

After I closed for the night and ran a comb through my hair, I hoofed it down to Edna's club, the Oasis, to see if she was back. There wasn't a soul in the place—it was locked up as tight as Dick's hatband. Even the street was empty. No one was nearby to ask what was going on. Since it was too far for me to walk to Edna's house, I went home.

The sheriff came back into the Bluebird the next morning and wanted to know if I had heard anything from her. Edna Love had been missing over a week. I had kind of lost track of the time.

"Have you talked to Johnny or Catfish?"

"Of course." The sheriff took a seat at the counter and leaned on his elbows.

I lifted the coffeepot, and he nodded his head.

"I haven't been by her house. When you told me she was gone, I thought she had planned a trip and forgot to tell me."

Sheriff blew a rivulet across the coffee, and the steam wandered away. He drank a big gulp.

"I'm gonna have to close down the laundromat, I guess. We can't keep letting old Clubby have access to her money. Even if he does live there."

"Well, do whatever you think is best. She's gonna be pissed when she comes back and she's lost income. Not to mention what all the women are gonna do without a washing machine."

I swear that men don't think about anybody but themselves.

The sheriff shook his head. "I guess I could get somebody to check on the deposits. I don't have time to run a dang laundromat, though."

He downed the rest of the coffee. How does he drink it so hot? He threw down a dollar as he stomped out.

I was getting a little worried about Edna. But, you know, her life is not exactly an open book.

When I can't sleep at night, the rooftop calls me. That night, I took some time to look at the stars and check on the moon, rising in the east, but slender in the first quarter with a bright star to the right.

First quarter moons signify beginnings, I think.

I wish I could just tilt the moon over and pour its power into my mouth. We spend nights staring at the moon as we search for her appearance. She reassures us and reminds us that some things never fail us. Even during the day, she rides hidden underneath the sun's brightness.

When she goes dark, I miss her. Yet I know she will reappear. Her steadiness reassures me. We humans are not so constant. We may float in and out of people's lives outside our orbits. But the moon always returns. She reveals both her sides—dark and radiant. I suppose if the moon has two faces, then it follows that we do, too.

What was beginning here in Nuanz? Edna was gone but not too far, I hoped. Something was hanging over us here.

7

Edna and the Stranger

When a stranger comes to town, he or she is usually observed from a distance for a while. In a small town, folks may be polite, but they are taking your measure. Some prejudge strangers by the way they talk, their physical appearance, or their attitude. The people in Nuanz have their own way of treating strangers when they move here. I know. I was a stranger on that day in April when I wandered into Love's Launderette and found it was easy to lay low in Nuanz. Edna Love made sure I was taken care of.

There's a distance, though, if you're not born in a certain place. I am sure there are so many "foreigners" in the cities that a stranger coming to town is no big deal. But in a small town like Nuanz, people notice when someone comes to town and stays. I had been here long enough and gotten into and out of enough trouble that I was mostly accepted. But let there be no doubt I would never be fully accepted. You had to be born here to really belong. As a matter of fact, it was preferable that your parents and even grandparents had been here for a very long time.

When I went to Mr. Frank Bob's funeral with Edna, the preacher added at the end, "He'd lived here fifty years, and he was almost one of us." They may say that one day at my funeral.

Now, if your family owns some land, that seals the deal. That's a Southern thing. There were plenty of people here who had money. But the real royalty owned land—that is, farmland. You might live in a shotgun house with a bare yard and old rundown cars. But if you owned some land, you had a certain reverence bestowed upon you.

So even if the "new" people in town had lived here for forty years and ran a prosperous business, if they didn't own their own piece of ground, then it didn't count. You could just go so far in Nuanz without owning land. Why? Well, as they say—you know the good Lord ain't making no more of it. That's why poor little widow women and sour old men might not seem to have much of anything, but if they wanted to lord it over somebody or subtly put you in your place, they could say, "My farm check came in today." Or they'd say, "We're putting part of the farm in set-aside for a year."

When a stranger comes to town, he may think he's gonna be the big fish in a little pond. He may feel like strutting around like a banty rooster, but he doesn't know the real power brokers are laughing up their sleeves at him and biding their time on their grandpappy's land.

This really had us going last year when a man with a funny last name bought the Albert Stewart house on the outskirts of town. Three moving vans from Chicago took over a week to unload. Mr. Salvatorre brought a woman with him who looked like an exotic gypsy with black hair and eyes and lots of gold jewelry. She had a different last name, too. Neither one wore a wedding band, and he introduced her as Lydia Mancini. Again, one of those names that ends in a vowel. She said little and kept to herself. Sometimes we wouldn't see her for weeks. But she added to the mystery.

They took over a month to move everything in. A large Mayflower Movers truck would pull into their circular drive and unload for a day or two. Then, a few days later, another would appear. The house was a Victorian white frame with three floors and an attic, tall ceilings, and multiple fireplaces. There was a downstairs porch and two balconies on the upper floors. They were going to fill the big house with furniture and knickknacks galore.

No one could figure out why this couple moved to Nuanz. The first bit of news came from their neighbors. Mrs. Jackson had taken a cake and a box of cookies over but was met at the door and not asked in. The women from the Welcome Wagon tried to make an entry. They knocked and knocked on the doors, but no one would ever come. They left baskets of goodies and notes, but no one ever answered. Even Mr. Gordon couldn't get more than a yes or no—or no, thank you—out of them. The mayor had met Mr. Salvatorre, and the real estate guy, Rosco Smiley, was acquainted with him, but they didn't know much.

That was last July. Finally, the building inspector let it slip that Mr. Salvatorre had bought the old Murphy Funeral Home on the east corner of Depot Street. The property consisted of one of the oldest brick homes in Nuanz, a carriage house that held the caskets and embalming rooms, and a chapel with fake stained-glass windows. The property looked abandoned and forlorn. Rosco was happy to sell that white elephant, too.

Sure enough, a sign was hung over the front entrance—Salvatorre Antique Gallery and Auction. We were all aflutter.

Soon, Edna Love appeared at the Bluebird Cafe with Mr. Salvatorre and introduced him around. There was a bit of unease at first. His accent was thick, and we hated to keep asking him what he said. The men nodded their heads and proceeded to talk around him. But he came in for coffee several days in a row until they seemed to expect him to join them at the back table. He always brought a *New York Times* and would sit at the counter while he drank his first cup of coffee and read over the front page. Sometimes he would get up and join the men. Sometimes he would go back to his business. He seemed nice enough.

I liked the way he said my name as *Mee-shah.* Coming out of his mustached mouth, my name seemed to belong to someone foreign and mysterious. Whenever he and Edna sat together, they acted like old friends. There was a vibe underneath their interaction that I was afraid to stand too near. But when he brought his girlfriend, he showered her with attention.

We couldn't figure out why Mr. Salvatorre had come all the way to Nuanz from way up north to open an antique shop. Who would drive to Nuanz to buy antiques? We were curious but didn't know enough to ask the right questions. But, boy, could we dream what might be going on!

Soon, Mr. Salvatorre was more at ease with us and vice versa. Still, the men never came out and asked him what was going on.

As usual, Edna knew more than anyone else. Every time she learned a fact or two, she shared with us. His full name was Guido Salvatorre, but we soon learned to call him Mr. S. He was short and stocky, with a dark complexion, big brown eyes, and wavy black hair that he combed straight back.

We tried to be indifferent, but we were intrigued with him. We learned that he was shipping antiques in from all over the world and planned on having live auctions here. We could not figure out what Nuanz, Tennessee, had to offer this stranger, but he certainly had brought some newness to our ordinary lives.

Edna asked me to go with her to Mr. S's gallery after he moved in. The two-story, brick house sprawled over a corner lot just a couple of blocks from the court square. There was a balcony on the second floor and a front porch beneath that. Attached to the side was a newer brick building with a ramp and double doors. When we walked up the sidewalk, Edna pointed to the building that was the funeral chapel. "The Murphys added that back in the '30s. But the house itself is about as old as the town of Nuanz."

From the outside, the house was in fine shape. It had two chimneys on each end. Edna rang the bell, and as we waited, she tapped her foot and glanced across the street at the Episcopal church.

"I haven't been in that church ever. They have kneeling benches you have to get up and down a hundred times during a service, they say." She shook her head. "I couldn't do all of that genuflecting stuff."

Suddenly, the door opened, and there stood a slight woman with bleached blond hair and an apron that reached down to her ankles. She stared at us. "Can I help you? We are not open today."

"Guido asked us to come by. Is he in?"

She shrugged and turned back into the hallway. Edna stepped in and pulled me with her. The woman walked to the end of the hall, opened the door, and disappeared. Then Mr. S came through the door.

"Hello, Edna. Welcome to Salvatorre Antique Gallery and Auction."

"Why, thank you. This is Meshac from the cafe."

"Of course, she pours my coffee just like I like it."

I tried not to mumble. He kept talking as we followed him into a large dining room and living room crowded with dark, ornate furniture. Paintings and lamps were everywhere. I sniffed money and oldness.

"Come back to the storage area. I have something I want you to see."

The double doors opened to a large, well-lit, square room that must have been where they kept the bodies. I didn't see any corpses, but the odor of embalming fluid drifted like you always smell at funeral homes. White sheeting covered rows of tables with glass bowls, wooden cabinets, and boxes underneath and stowed on top. The far table held framed prints, mirrors, and lamps. On the wall behind were bigger paintings and old family portraits. Mr. S unlocked a small case and pulled out a tiny canvas wrapped in oilcloth. He motioned us nearer.

"Are you interested in paintings?"

I didn't say a word. Edna sighed. "I had a friend once who had some real art. What is this?"

He handed her the small painting, full of blues, greens, and pinks, a scene by a river.

"Who do you think did this?"

"Where did you get it?" Edna asked, like that might give her a hint.

He smiled and turned the painting over. There was a sticker that had some writing I couldn't make out. He read the name of the gallery, Mencino Italia.

"I found it buried in a trunk I bought there. Have you ever heard of the artist Renoir?"

Of course, I hadn't, but Edna seemed to know it.

"This is a Renoir?"

"Well, it looks like a sample, maybe a plan for something bigger. Look at the colors. See the brush strokes?"

They both leaned over closer to look.

"So how old is this?"

"Oh, probably close to 100 years old."

"Is it real?"

Mr. S stared at the tiny canvas. "I think so, but I can't prove it yet."

Edna was impressed and quiet. We wandered around, and Mr. S showed us several more items. There was a stuffed peacock, a copper teapot on a stand, portraits of sour-looking old women, layers of rugs, old letters, books, brass trays, and candlesticks everywhere. He unlocked a big wooden chifforobe and wrapped a long, velvet stole around me. It was soft and smelled of mothballs. He offered Edna a perfume bottle and asked me if I saw anything I would like to have. I told him I would be afraid I would break it. He laughed and walked on.

We came to a large set of double doors. He hesitated and then abruptly turned around, serious now. "That's where the good stuff is."

Then he smiled. "Tell your friends that I have some fine antiques here. They are for sale for a price. After the monthly auction, we will ship a lot to buyers on the East Coast and then bring in more merchandise."

Edna and I finished the tour, and my head swam with all the stuff I had seen. I still didn't understand why Mr. Salvatorre had come down here from Chicago to sell these fine antiques.

But after that visit, Mr. S came into the cafe more often, and he was friendlier as he drank his coffee. Many times, he and Edna arrived together. They laughed and talked as if they were old friends. Edna acted younger when she was around Mr. S. I couldn't figure it out.

Mr. Salvatorre became a regular at the Bluebird. He and his lady friend came in at night every so often. He left her when he went on buying trips for weeks. By this time, Salvatorre Antique Gallery and Auction was going big guns. He always left a nice tip at the cafe, and his employees talked like they were happy with their work and pay. He used both locals and some strangers who came in occasionally. We had accepted him and his new enterprise. Even the men were friendly to him and always listened whenever he spoke.

When a stranger comes to town, though, there is sometimes that false honeymoon until the truth comes out. We should have known there would be trouble. We should have known.

Edna continued to take a special interest in Mr. S and his lady friend despite the warnings from the Welcome Wagon women. Edna called them "The Tale Waggers." As always, Edna was eager to share any gossip with the Bluebird regulars, and I was always hanging out with my big ears open. Today, she had a tableful of gossips waiting for the latest scoop.

Edna confided, "Mr. S has auction houses in Chicago, Connecticut, Virginia, and out west. He thought Memphis would be a great place to open another one. Then, somehow, he heard about our quaint little town."

Edna brought her coffee cup to her lips, and her eyes danced above the rim. "He likes the old homes we have and the Southern way of living. He claims people will drive hundreds of miles to come to a real live antique auction."

She pursed her lips together and shrugged her shoulders. "Can't hurt us to have a little extra business in town, can it?"

We nodded our heads, although in our hearts, we just didn't know for sure. But we were willing to give him a chance—kind of.

Finally, Salvatorre Antique Gallery and Auction was ready for its first live auction on the first weekend in November. Trucks had been unloading for weeks, and we figured the place was stuffed. Boy Blue and Sun Man had headed up a group of locals to help unload. Mr. S paid good money, and nobody broke anything. When we asked what all was in there, we got no straight answers. Edna called on Lydia a time or two but never shared much news that was useful for us commoners.

During the first auction, we stood around with our mouths dropped open. People came from everywhere. They got there early Saturday morning, and we nearly ran out of breakfast by seven o'clock. They drove big, fine cars and shiny pickup trucks with trailers behind them. Some filled their gas tanks all the way, and they wanted something to eat. A few even rented rooms at the Nuanz Motor Inn. We couldn't believe it. Our cash registers were ringing all day long.

The auction started at ten and went on until five. People stood outside under the big oak trees that had been there since the beginning of Nuanz over 200 years ago. Those trees had never shaded anything like this before.

I stood in the back after lunch was over and watched the bidding. Big dollars were flying out of people's pockets with no thought at all. I made sure to stand as still as I could. No bidding from this young lady. But it was neat to watch the items they brought out on the stand. The auctioneer's voice was loud over the speaker, but you could tell he knew what he was doing. There wasn't much hesitancy in the bidding. Two or three big-time collectors battled over a few items.

After the first auction, the town settled into accepting Mr. S and Miss Lydia. When they came into the cafe, either the Nuanz Literary Club women or the Liars' Table men always made a point of talking to them, even if it was nothing more than to say, "How are things going?" or "Good to see you folks." Mr. S softened, too.

Edna was in the middle of things. I teased her about Mr. S and told her Lydia would probably scratch her eyes out. That didn't faze Edna in the least.

Mr. S's auction house was bringing money to our local economy. No one wanted to discourage that. But we couldn't quite figure out what he was doing here. After a while, the questions died down, but the doubts lingered.

In late November, Edna asked me to go back to see Mr. S again. I had a day off and went with her. I could tell she and Mr. S were friendlier, almost as if they were longtime friends. When we got there this time, we went in the back door where the kitchen was, and the lady who worked for him was pricing glassware on the kitchen counter. The countertops and the long table in the center of the room were filled with cut-glass bowls, trays, and glasses. The woman inspected each one and entered them into inventory.

She greeted Edna—that's how I knew Edna had been here frequently. After we chatted, she said, "Mr. S is in the office."

Edna and I started toward the front of the house. The hallway was dark, and the carpet was so thick you couldn't hear our footsteps. I heard Mr. S's voice before we got to the door. He was on the phone, and his words had an edge to them:

"I told you I needed them on Thursday, and they have not arrived yet."

He paused.

"Doesn't matter. I told you."

Silence. Then his voice was quiet, but the words were distinct.

"I will send him the day after tomorrow. Be there."

Edna knocked on the open door; he turned, and his eyes were dark and narrow. Then he instantly broke into a smile and waved us in. He dismissed the caller and hung up.

"Oh, Edna, come in and sit down. How are you, Mesha?"

I loved his accent. He reminded me of Clark Gable. My heart fluttered. I couldn't help it.

"We don't want to bother you, but we had a few minutes. You told me you had something you wanted me to see. "

He laughed and folded his arms. "Oh, I see I have a new antique shopper on my hands."

"Well, now, I don't know about that. But I do like some of this stuff, you know." Edna's voice had that business-like but sultry tone. I don't know how she does that.

Mr. S. stood up. "Come on back to the chapel."

We followed him through the double doors into the funeral chapel, which still had its eerie lights but no benches now. The room was packed. I couldn't take in everything; there was so much.

He took Edna over to a small case and unlocked the doors. He took out a fancy crystal bottle. "Here's that French perfume bottle I wanted you to see. "

They began oohing and aahing, and I wandered through the aisles. There was a musty smell that said, "I am old, but I am worth something." In the corner was a tall cabinet with glass doors. Inside, there were all kinds of figurines. Fancy delicate ballerinas posed in different ways. Figurines of queens, nuns, and priests. At the bottom were some animals, an elephant and a giraffe. They looked heavy, like they were out of stone or metal. I bent closer to look at them. They looked real enough to touch. Mr. S walked up behind me.

"Ah, you see the Bugatti?"

I straightened up. "What?"

"The animal sculptures there. They are by Rembrandt Bugatti."

I shrugged my shoulders. "They are very nice. Looks like they are ready to move or pounce."

He bent over and unlocked the case. He pulled out the giraffe almost reverently.

"Bugatti was the youngest son of the Bugatti family in Italy." He held up the giraffe for me to see. "The Bugatti car maker? Ever heard of them?"

"No, sir."

"It's not important, but this son never got into the car business. He was an artist. This is his work."

I stared at the piece he had pulled out. "It looks pretty good to me, I guess."

"Well, the artist is the typical poor little rich boy. Yes, he was named after Rembrandt—the Rembrandt. You see, he became a sculptor. He was lonely, and he spent time observing the animals at the zoo. That is why his work is about animals like these: lions, tigers, giraffes, elephants."

Mr. S shook his head. "Of course, when he killed himself, his artwork skyrocketed in value. I have six pieces now."

"Are they for sale?"

"Not really. I like them too much. My grandmother knew the Bugattis personally. She said he was a lonely man who saw beauty all around him."

I loved looking at the long neck and the knobby knees of the giraffe. "That is so neat that your grandmother knew him and sad, too, that he didn't have any people friends."

"I know. But maybe that is why his art is so good . . . and so valuable." He ran his fingers down the giraffe's neck.

Edna was ready to go. "Come, Mesha, let's check out. Is there anything you want?"

I couldn't help myself. "Well, what about this giraffe?"

She peered inside the cabinet and then laughed. "That one's probably way out of my price range."

Mr. S laughed. "Maybe not."

They both exchanged some kind of look, but I dismissed it as more of Edna's flirtatious ways. She was like that—if there's a man with a heartbeat around, she's gonna flirt.

8

Finer Things

As we settled into that late winter, the dark days brought some doubt, fear, and careful considerations. I was enjoying myself more than I had at any time since I had fled to Nuanz three years ago. I liked Mr. S and his antiques.

I don't know much about the finer things in life. I barely finished high school. Growing up, I didn't have a lot of books at my house, but I had some good teachers who stirred me to be better than I was.

Mrs. Bledsoe, my sixth-grade teacher, read to us every afternoon after lunch. Her voice sent me to unknown places. She read a poem about a river, a sword, and a princess, maybe one about Sir Lancelot called "The Lady of the Lake." I remember the gist of that story still, which was that Lady emerging from the bottom of the lake holding that sword over her head.

We would beg Mrs. Bledsoe to read more. Sometimes she would finish one more chapter. My high school English teacher made us read *Great Expectations.* Poor little Pip was as poor as I was. Those pages that were filled with so many words helped me to drift away from my real life. Then there was the poem "The Tyger" by William Blake. The words "Tyger, Tyger burning bright" would float into my brain at odd moments. I could see Miss Arnold standing by the window reading those words that floated over our sleepy heads after lunch. For those teachers, I will always be thankful.

Plus, thank God for the library. I do know my way around there. That was always a refuge for me in Wicket. A good place to hide from my mother and George. A good place to think and read about faraway places.

When Mr. S showed me those statues, naturally, I went to the library to find out whatever I could. The next day off, I trudged over there and read about Rembrandt Bugatti. Yes, he was a famous sculptor from Italy. He was thin and pale in the black and white photos in the artist book. He wore a wide-brimmed straw hat and loose-flowing shirts and pants.

The name Rembrandt made me think of our Rem—Remington Moore. I wondered if he'd heard of Mr. Bugatti. I wanted to know if those sculptures were real and if they were worth anything. Well, guess what? That statue of the giraffe looked just like the one Mr. S had and was worth about $50,000. Wow. I wondered if that was real or not, and if it was, why on earth did Mr. S have it down here in Nuanz, Tennessee?

I decided to pay a little more attention to Mr. S the next time he was in the cafe.

9

My Gang—Edna, Grace, Queen, and Joe

One thing I like about my life now are the people in it. After that first year here in Nuanz, I didn't know if I would stick around or not. Luckily, I did. The people I knew from the cafe had my back. There was no reason for them to take me in, but they did. Grace Robinson needed a friend as much as I did. Queen Esther and I were finding unfamiliar ground could be safe and comforting. I missed having a family, but coming here forced me to see things differently. I tried to hang on and understand each bump in the road.

My gang, as I called them, consisted of Edna Love, Grace Nell Robinson, Queen Esther, and Joe. Each one filled a missing part of my life here, and I tried to give back to each one. A girl could do worse, right?

I know that when people see me with Queen, they can't help but think how opposite we are. Queen has dark brown hair stacked around her high cheekbones and arched eyebrows. Her skin is a perfect milk-chocolate brown. I have rag-tag, blondish hair and deep blue eyes. She's taller than me, but my hips sway when I move without even trying. Really.

Grace is young and alone, being raised by her Aunt Virginia, and I understand exactly what that's like after I rescued myself from old George's abuse. Edna Love—and I'm not exaggerating—runs the town. Joe is my boyfriend when he is back from his job; he understands me, most of the time anyway. And Queen Esther gave me my first ride back to Nuanz from the protest and became my friend forever.

One day, Grace stopped by the cafe. "Hey, Squirt, where have you been?" I asked.

She smiled and ducked her head. "Nowhere."

We sat down on the steps to the street.

"How come you haven't been by to worry me to death then?"

She tried to keep from smiling. "It's kind of hard to get in with those big old doors all locked up." She pointed back at the Friedman Building.

"I guess you want me to give you a key?"

"Wouldn't hurt, or at least hide one somewhere."

I shook my head. But in truth, she did have a harder time hooking up with me now. At the Nuanz Motor Inn, I usually sat outside if the weather permitted or hung out with Loretta in the office. Grace knew where I was then. She did have friends now, and she was thirteen years old. But I felt a need to protect her still.

"I don't really want to give you a key to my apartment, but you could tell me when you're coming."

"Oh, that's too much trouble. At least get a couple of chairs or a bench for us to sit on and watch the traffic go by."

"Well, I might do that. Although I might have some hangers-on bothering me then."

She laughed. "Who wants to hang on to you?"

"You'd be surprised!" I elbowed her and rolled my eyes.

"What are you doing this summer once school is out?"

"Well, last summer I had a babysitting job with the Fishers over on Church Street."

"That's nice. How many kids?"

"Supposed to be two, but lots of times the other kids on the street came over, too."

"Do they pay you by the hour or by the kid?"

She laughed. "I wish. But it wasn't too bad. This year, it's just every other week, though."

"The money comes in handy, doesn't it?"

She nodded her head and stretched her legs out. Her toenails were painted a bright red.

"How's Aunt Virginia?"

"Meaner than hell."

"So she's just the same then?"

"Yes. She falls asleep in her recliner every night by eight and snores like a buzzsaw."

"But you stay safe, right?"

She hesitated before she answered, "I try my best."

We both watched two cars drive around the square.

"Have you seen all that stuff they are hauling into the auction house?"

"Yep. They have something coming in there all the time."

"I wonder if they need any help there."

"Doing what?"

"I don't know. Unpacking stuff. Cleaning and dusting."

I shook my head. "Are you good at that?"

"Pretty good, I think."

"Well, I will say something to Mr. S the next time he's in the cafe."

"Thanks. I gotta go now." She jumped up before I could pat her on the back.

"I will try and find us something to sit on outside and watch the world go by."

"That would be nice."

She grinned and left. I wandered back inside. I wiped down the counter and filled the sugar canisters. I was in the back of the restaurant when the bell jingled, and Queen opened the door. I was the only one around.

"Hey, girl. Whatcha doing? Come on in."

I walked up to the front. "Want a cup of coffee or a glass of tea?"

Queen sat at the front counter. I eased behind the counter, reached into the cooler for a scoop of ice, and set out two glasses of tea. I pulled up my stool as she sat about where Miss Florence and her daughter were when they were the first black people to sit here for a cup of coffee; that felt like a hundred years ago.

Queen is a good-looking, young black woman. She has her own agenda that sometimes is just about her but many times is about finding her own way. She is probably the closest thing to a friend my age that I have here. Plus, she has a car. People look at us funny when we're together, but we are used to that.

"What's on your mind today, Queen Esther?"

The more I learned as I hung out with Queen, the more I realized what I didn't know. There is a whole underworld of blackness that white people know nothing about. Our white ears and hearts hear nothing and feel nothing for many of our black citizens. Then something slaps us in our smug little faces—like the murder of little Noah Johnson in the whites-only swimming pool. That one event changed a few white hearts. I know it did mine.

Without saying so, Queen and I tried to understand the other parts of our two worlds. Since I was an outcast by not being born here, I could blunder into some situations and plead ignorance—easily done. But I liked to think that even though my upbringing was not intended to make me see others in a different light, what I knew and thought about lent me a different kind of knowledge. That helped me discover some things about the world and about myself.

"Oh, nothing much, Mesha. What's going on with you?"

"Working my fingers to the bone is all."

"When's that boyfriend of yours getting back in town?"

She couldn't care less when Joe was getting back in town. "I don't know. Maybe this week sometime. Why?"

She took a long sip of iced tea. "I got a free night coming up, thought maybe we might get in some trouble somewhere."

"Where and when?"

Queen laughed, just as I knew she would. "Oh, Mesha. You just won't do now."

She finished her tea and made to pay me.

"It's on the house."

"Miss Florence was asking about you. You oughta come by and have lunch with her down at Rem's."

"I know. I've been craving some good food."

"Well, come on down. But behave." And out the door she sashayed.

My boyfriend Joe and I were getting along fine. I had come a long way. I was grateful that Joe treated me as well as he did. At the same time, I was still cautious and tried to keep my feet on the ground. But it was hard when your heart ratcheted up and you wanted to feel somebody next to you.

Edna had perked up a bit. She was making short trips to Memphis about twice a month. That had helped her state of mind. Spring had officially arrived, bringing hope that everything was going to be better now. Sometimes you have to let things work out on their own. I kept an eye out for Edna and tried to stand ready if she needed me.

It was meatloaf night at the Bluebird. When you're in the business of serving people, you learn a lot about human nature. People everywhere like to complain. If they can't find something real to complain about, then they invent something. When you work with the public, that's one of the things you have to get used to.

The most frequent complaint I got at the Bluebird was about the menu. The older men gathered at two tables pulled together and called it the Liars' Table. They loved to act like they'd never been in there before.

It would usually start when one of the men would ask what the special was tonight. This was while they were staring at the menu as if they'd never seen it. Then we had a routine we would go through something like this:

I would say, "Gee, I don't know." Then I'd turn and point at the calendar on the wall. "Let's see, this is Wednesday. Is that right?" That's when the complaining man starts to grin.

I continue, "If it's Wednesday—hmmm, I might have to double-check with Mr. Rob, but I think it's meatloaf, mashed potatoes, green beans, and rolls. Pie is extra."

Then you get the hemming and hawing excuses. "I don't know. I'm not that hungry." Or, "The last time I ate meatloaf, I had heartburn."

That's my favorite. That's when I lean over and give him the look. "Then don't order the meatloaf. We put an extra dose of heartburn in it today."

The first time I said that, Mr. Hardaway laughed so hard that he spit out his iced tea all over the table. That little routine made those lonely old men a little happier. I aim to please.

10

Settling In

I wouldn't say every day was the same, but mostly they were except for the cafe menu. The Liars' Table was always full on Wednesdays. The Ladies' Library Book Club came in on Tuesdays. The Nuanz Literary Club came in whenever one of their hostesses couldn't fix chicken casserole and Jell-O fruit salad lunch at their home. I think they got tired of casseroles.

If anyone new came in, people stared at them. Then everybody would recall their manners and get busy with their food.

I never saw Mr. S's lady friend up close except when he brought her into the cafe for a meal at night. He'd leave town frequently, and his lady friend huddled in the big old house. You could see her sitting on the porch when you went by, but she never invited anyone to come sit with her.

The auctions were held one weekend a month. Some townspeople went to the first ones just to see what was going on. Mrs. Buford said they had some nice antiques, but everything was way too high for her. The judge's wife, who bragged about how much money she had as the only daughter of a big cotton farmer, would casually mention buying a vase or lamp or an antique rocker there. Most of Depot Street would fill with vans and covered square trucks on auction days. Most license plates were from out of state. But Mr. S had a nice relationship with the Bank of Nuanz and began to be accepted more and more in our town. A little mystery never hurt anybody. That mysterious stranger was slowly becoming one of us.

When Mr. S came into the cafe that morning by himself and sat at the counter, I had gotten to know him fairly well. I took his order, and when it was plated, I said to him casually, "Have you heard from Edna lately?"

He raised his eyebrows. "No, why?"

I stumbled a bit. "She just hasn't been around this week."

He shrugged his shoulders and reached for the salt. "Does she usually do this?"

"Maybe for a few days she might disappear. But this time is a long hiatus."

I tried not to stare at him, but I couldn't help myself. He nodded, then turned his fork over and cut up his fried eggs into precise, triangular pieces. "I can't remember exactly when I last saw her."

He lifted his fork for the first bite. "I am sure she'll turn up."

That sounded dismissive, so I went back to my waitressing duties. When Mr. S paid his bill later, he lingered there as if he needed to say something. I stood still and waited.

"Let me know if you need any help with Edna."

I didn't know what he meant by that. I said, "Sure, thanks."

He went out the door. Sometimes I felt my breath catch in my throat when he turned his dark eyes on me.

Saturdays at the Bluebird

Saturdays at the Bluebird had a different rhythm from the weekdays. This Saturday was the first weekend in May with the weather feeling like summer. Monday was what we called First Monday, following the first full weekend of the month, and was a special time set aside for yard sales, flea markets, bake sales, and hanging out. Everyone started setting up on Friday before First Monday, and early selling started on Saturday. The First Monday in May was always large because the weather beckoned you to come out and see what your neighbors had to sell.

Who didn't like to rummage through stacks of 45 records, *Saturday Evening Posts*, and discarded clothes? Church ladies had bake sales, and old men traded knives and sold ax handles. Mrs. Berry always had a box of her dead husband's shoes. He'd been gone more than five years, but every First Monday, Mrs. Berry was there to size up random men's feet. She could spot a size 8D a block away. Miss Mildred always paraded through with her ancient Persian cat on its long, pink satin ribbon, then fussed when a dog ran Kitty up a tree. Iron skillets and gourd dippers always went early.

At least once a season, Sarah Parker would forget and sell her granddaddy's Confederate cap, then cry when she realized it was gone. We would be on the lookout until somebody found it on a young boy's head and bought it back again. From shot glasses and teacups to fishing tackle and little red wagons, there was always something for everybody at First Monday. Edna told me the custom began back in the days of horse and mule trading and changed as the town and people changed.

It was always a bigger day for us at the cafe. Mr. Rob taught me early that you don't want to overthink those big days. Lots of times, your big plans don't work out, and you're stuck with too many quarts of milk and fruit getting soft.

For this weekend, I had ordered extra pork chops, and we had a special listed underneath the Page Jewelers clock on the wall: First Monday special plate—pork chops, creamed potatoes, succotash, and a roll for $2.50. Peach cobbler cost extra.

The crowd was constant from early breakfast through lunch. By midafternoon, we had finally slowed down, but there were still lots of people in town. People liked to park their cars around the square, stroll from store to store, and visit. Maybe get caught up on the latest gossip. You had to watch if you left your unlocked car for long. Mrs. Whittaker would climb in, and it would take forever to talk her out of it.

Farmers came to town if they weren't planting. The barbershops stayed open late. Usually, the theater had Gene Autry or Roy Rogers for both morning and afternoon matinees. Then they would finish up with a double feature on Saturday night.

If you stood outside the cafe, you could hear the auctioneer at Salvatorre Antique Gallery and Auction standing on the flatbed truck next to the funeral home chapel. He had a big crowd this weekend for his auction.

I was watching outside when Grace emerged from a crowd of girls. She grinned at me as she led the group toward the front door.

I couldn't get used to her new look. She was so tall now, thin, with shiny, blond hair down to her shoulders. This didn't even seem like the same kid who had shadowed me that first summer I moved here. We had been through a lot, the two of us.

Grace was changing as she sailed past that gawky, long-legged stage between child and teen. Her attitude ranged between hostile and sarcastic. That helped her fit in with a group of girls who weren't the most popular but not the dregs of society, either. She still felt some kind of responsibility for me. I tried not to smother her, but I would always be there if she needed me. That motherly feeling was certainly foreign to me, though.

When her friends settled in the front booth, Grace played the waitress role. I could hear her voice: "Okay, what do y'all want?"

She got the head count of how many milkshakes and how many Cokes, and watching her stand there with her hand on her hip, I could tell she relished this bossy role. She came over and gave me the full order.

"Yes, ma'am, I'll have it right out." I snapped a quick salute.

She rolled her eyes at me. "Whatever." It was good to see her acting like a normal kid.

"What are you up to today?" I asked.

"Nothing, just hanging out. We might catch the matinee, but we're mainly just hanging out."

"Are you looking for some no-account boys?"

"No way," she said, with that little-girl smirk that reminded me of a few years back.

I brought the girls their orders and drifted back to the counter to review the menu for Sunday dinner and check the supplies.

I couldn't quite settle down all afternoon. We closed around nine, and I decided to walk down to the Oasis to see if Edna was in town. I didn't even bother changing my clothes before I walked to Depot Street and down the two blocks to the club. I could see the palm tree neon light glowing in the window, and for a moment, I thought Edna was back. But when I got nearer, there were no cars or indoor lights. The neon palm trees swayed, and that old yellow cat lapped water from the drainpipe out back. Guess she's missing Edna, too. This was highly unusual on a First Monday weekend for the Oasis to be closed. Edna was out of town more than she was in town. Those trips to Memphis were getting more frequent.

There were cars whizzing by over the railroad tracks, and I could feel the nearness of others, but I couldn't see anyone. I walked up the hill past the bank and the supermarket. I came to the corner of the block, and as I rounded the corner, I could hear voices near the bank across the street. I leaned into the shadows. Two men stood beside a black sedan. Their words were lost on me until one of them raised his voice.

"What do you mean you don't know?"

"I don't know. She could be anywhere."

The first man grabbed hold of the skinny one and pushed him against the car. My heart jumped up in my throat.

"That's not what I'm asking. We need to find her now."

The other guy straightened his hat and took a step away from the first man. "I've asked around everywhere."

"Well, get in her business and see if there's anything going on there." They stood silent for a minute. I didn't know if I should tiptoe down the street or stay where I was. They thought they were completely alone.

"Hop in the car and we'll ride by." They piled in, one in the front seat and the other in the back. The driver started the car. They rolled down the block and turned west.

The moon had risen over the long, dusty roof of the feed company on the east side of the square. Moonlight always made things look better. This moon was a lopsided second quarter, with its yellowness fading quickly. A lone star hung not too far south; maybe that was Venus. The courthouse clock struck, and I counted the dongs—one, two, three, four, five. Well, that was about half what it should have been. Not bad.

I unlocked the downstairs double doors to the Friedman Building, locked them again, and walked up to my apartment. I opened the windows wide, and a slight breeze blew the curtains. They rustled as I drew my chair to the kitchen table. Were those men plotting something big, or did I even hear things right?

Girl, you need to find something to fill your life. Calm the hell down, I thought. I turned on the radio and searched for a late-night DJ taking requests. Static was all I could get. Story of my life, huh.

Between Grace and Edna choosing their own paths, and Joe, my sometime boyfriend, still gone for weeks on his riverboat job, I wasn't left with much but the Bluebird Cafe.

I have a few regrets. Who doesn't? There's a lingering lukewarm revenge surfacing from time to time from my past life, but I am doing okay.

Car lights pulled me to the window, and that same car crept around the square, slowed in front of the cafe, and then turned right down Highway 104.

Edna, hon, where are you?

PART II
THE LURE

Meow

The following Tuesday, Edna reappeared at my counter as if all was normal again.

"Look what the cat drug in."

She smiled and took her seat. I stood there with my hands on the counter, waiting for her opening line. She grinned.

"Okay, where have you been?" I didn't even pretend to be cleaning the counter. I zeroed in on Edna. She patted the back of her French twist.

"Around." She shrugged her shoulders like a teenager.

"Where around?"

"Memphis. I thought I told you."

"No, you didn't tell anybody. You missed First Monday weekend."

"I got caught up in some things."

She dropped her eyes to the countertop like she was trying to be coy. I knew her game.

"If you don't want to tell me, I'm not gonna beg."

"Good. Pour me a cup of coffee. Fresh, please."

I set up her coffee and waited to see if she would let me in on it all. Her eyes sparkled like she'd had another good time.

"Edna, you look better than you did a few months ago."

"Why, what do you mean? I always look good."

"You know. When you were grousing around about wanting to fall in love again." I waited to see if she was going to talk or evade my prying.

Edna studied her painted nails and then studied me. "Well, things are better right now for me."

"And why is that?" That ought to get her going.

She smiled and shook her head. Then she said, "I may be making some big changes in the next few months."

"Like what?"

"Like getting rid of this old town and moving on."

"Now where in the world would you move to? You know you'd miss Nuanz."

She had to be kidding.

"Mesha, there's a whole world out there. If I am going to explore it, I better get busy."

I nodded my head and watched as the Alexanders came in and slid into their booth.

"Hold on a minute." I took them their water and handed them the menus. They always want to study the menu like they've never seen it before.

"Give us a few minutes," the wife said.

"Sure."

Edna had turned halfway on her stool and stared out the big picture window.

"Do you want more coffee or a piece of chess pie?"

"No, hon. I am just fine. Gotta get back down to the Oasis and make a deposit from last night."

"Who is the man?" I watched her closely to see if she flinched.

"Whatcha mean?"

"There's gotta be a man involved in all this fancy exploring what's out there. I know you."

She raised one eyebrow and grinned. "He's about the finest thing I have ever run across."

"Whoa, Edna. Tell me about him."

She giggled. Really like a teenager. "He is so smooth. But not in a bad way. He is older than I am, but I can't tell how much. I don't know. He says the right thing and looks the right way when I am with him."

"Why don't you bring him around?"

"He's coming down soon, but he doesn't like to get too social."

"I guess he's got all he can handle with you."

"That's exactly what I told him." Then she said so low I had to lean closer, "There's something about him that . . ." She snapped her fingers. "Clicks, you know."

She had this look on her face that was so unlike Edna that I opened my mouth to say something sassy. Then I stopped, remembering that this was Edna Love.

"Well, as long as you are writing down all these secrets in your little black book, I won't press you right now."

She leaned back and laughed that wonderful, wheezy laugh that comes from the center of her big heart.

"Law, Mesha, you just won't do." She grabbed her purse, slung it over her shoulder, and turned toward the back of the Bluebird Cafe. Her eyes wandered over the crowd, and she made her way to the men's table to see if she still had it. They called out her name. She did.

As the afternoon wound down, I caught sight of Queen Esther strolling down the street. She rarely came into the cafe herself, so I met her outside.

Queen and I had become friends since the sit-in days at the lunch counter in Jackson. She had helped the black community in their efforts to integrate the lunch counter at the Bluebird. We were close to the same age and from different backgrounds, but we felt safe with each other. People gave us that look when they saw us talking to each other. We kind of prided ourselves on keeping people stirred up that way. Plus, she had a car, and I didn't.

"Hey, girl, where you going?"

She cut her eyes around at me with that perpetual badass look on her face. Then she grinned. "I'm going down to Rem's, where they serve real food."

"Can I go with you?"

Queen shook her head. "You're the wrong color, girl. You oughta know better than that."

I would have liked to hook my arm in hers and stroll on down the sidewalk, but I didn't. She waited to see if I really did want something.

"Have you talked to Edna lately?"

Her eyebrows raised an inch. "No. Should I?"

"I wondered if you had seen her since she got back."

"From where?"

"Memphis."

"Hmm." That's all I got from her.

"Do you know what's going on with her?"

Queen paused a little too long. "Naw, I ain't studying Miss Edna."

"Of course, I knew that."

She turned to walk on.

"Come by and sit out with me some time," I hollered at her.

She shook her head and threw up her skinny, black arm. "Yes, ma'am. Whatever you say."

Her laughter floated up the hill to me. I could nearly smell Miss Florence's fried chicken from there, I swear. We don't even try to compete with her chicken and greens at Rem's Place. Miss Florence and her brother, Remington Moore, were kind to me when I needed to sit and talk like regular folks. If it hadn't been for them, we would have never caught the man who murdered little Noah Johnson that first summer I lived in Nuanz.

I got busy then, clearing tables and jawing with Lolly. Mr. Rob was sitting out back with his chair leaned up against the wall. The sun cast its red and yellow light against the lingering blue sky. Enjoying the slight breeze, I threw out the mop water and hung the mop to dry.

"Mr. Rob, you about ready to call it a day?" He eased the chair down and put his feet on the ground.

"I reckon so." He threw the smoldering cigarette into the coffee can with the others and set it down beside the chair. He slowly stretched like an old, crippled cat.

"The days are getting longer."

"Too long for me."

"Oh, don't start that again. I don't feel sorry for you at all."

He frowned to hide the smile quivering at the corners of his mouth.

"You 'bout ready to buy me out?" He peered over his smudged glasses.

"Sure, let me go get that bundle of money underneath my mattress. Cash all right?"

He shook his head, coughed, and cleared his throat.

"You know, one of these days, you and me do need to make a deal."

"I thought we had a deal. You give me the Bluebird, and I will give you free coffee for a year."

He laughed this time. "Nope, I am holding out for apple pie, too."

"Well, I don't know about that."

Joe and the Moon

Joe sauntered into the Bluebird late that next Friday afternoon. His six weeks on the riverboat were over. Yes, I was glad to see him. Joe and I had an odd relationship. We both had our own lives to live. I tried to run him off several times, but he always came back for more. Thank God. I was lucky that way. He knew all about me, but we kept working things out.

He was tall and slim with just enough muscle to not look wimpy. You could tell he was used to physical labor. His broad shoulders and arms swung easily when he walked. When he smiled, the skin around his gray eyes crinkled. He had an intensity about certain things that surprised me.

I sat down on the edge of the work stool behind the counter, and he sat across from me. I wondered for a moment how both of us must look there. He was already tan from the early summer sun and the river breezes. I perched on the edge of my stool with knees drawn up, narrow shoulders, and sun-streaked, ordinary hair. His hair curled around his shirt collar. I had the urge to touch it but didn't. His eyes locked with mine. They seemed to like what they saw. Something about him just made me feel good.

I never could understand why Joe wanted to be with me, but I tried to enjoy what I could and go on.

"Hello, Mr. River Man. How are you today?"

"Doing okay. How's Miss Bluebird flitting around?"

"Still flitting. How long are you in town?"

"My usual." Then he turned around and gazed at the crowd. "What's the news?"

I gave him the low-down—First Monday going on, the Whittakers washing their feet in the courthouse fountain again, and Edna's secret getaways.

I could tell he was surprised about Edna but not so surprised about our regular life. He drummed his fingers on the counter, and his eyes wandered away.

"Do you want to go over to Jackson this weekend?"

I didn't quite understand the question. "What do you mean? Like for supper?"

"No, let's do something different," Joe said with an intensity I hadn't seen before.

"What?" I leaned closer to him.

"Let's go spend the weekend over there."

"Why?" I asked.

"Well, to do stuff."

"Like what?"

"You know. Go out. Go eat, go to a movie, hang out in a club and drink and dance."

I waited for him to say, "Oh, I was just kidding." He didn't.

"What's gotten into you?"

"Nothing."

"I can't all of a sudden take off and go spend a weekend away."

"Just think about it. If not this weekend, then the next?" He ended the sentence with a question mark.

"Is this supposed to be some kind of big deal?"

"No, but I been thinking . . . a lot. We've been together, whether you like it or not, for a couple of years now. I am ready to change some things."

"What do you mean?"

Joe glanced out the door, then back at me . . . and leaned over and kissed me right in front of God and the Bluebird Cafe. I swooned. I did. I heard somebody at the back say, "Would you look at those lovebirds?"

But I really didn't care at that point. Boy. I straightened myself and mumbled, "I have to check the locker for tomorrow."

He laughed. "I will come by tonight. What time do you get off work?"

"It's eight tonight."

"I will be here."

When he left, I couldn't get anything done. I was like crazy drunk or something. Just when I think I have everything under control, some crazy something like this happens. Now why on earth should I let a little ole kiss make me weak in the knees?

The afternoon slogged on. We were busy during supper, and that helped. When I got ready to close up at eight, Joe stood at the window and waved at me. He waited till the last customer left and I made up the deposit and put the cash drawer in the safe. When I stepped outside, I felt frazzled and greasy but excited, too.

"What do you want to do now?"

"Let's walk around the square and see what happens."

We started down the hill past the alley and Mr. Harwood's office. The lights in the back were on. We passed the rest of Lawyers Row, the dry cleaners, and the old dairy building. Then we walked toward the service station, the city water department, and over to Pierce's Pool Room. We went in for a couple of beers to see what was going on. None of the regulars were there, and we had an easy couple of hours, talking and drinking.

Joe decided to put some quarters in the jukebox. He picked Patsy Cline singing "Crazy," which was fine with me. Then he took my hand, pulled me close, and we swayed a little back and forth in that corner by the jukebox.

We walked south to the drinking fountain and splashed a bit on each other. The Confederate soldier statue loomed over us. Then we crossed the street and window-shopped at Friedman's Department Store and the five and dime. As we crossed the big intersection, I looked at the courthouse, standing proud like a grand old lady with the lights encircling the square. We went past Dr. McRee's office, the shoe store, the Bank of Nuanz, and City Drug Store with the soda fountain. They were all shuttered for the night. Then we crossed over to my block and the Friedman Building again.

By then, I was relaxed, and, yes, happy.

"Come on up, and we'll play the radio real loud."

Joe laughed. I unlocked the double doors, and since there wasn't a light on in the second-floor offices, it was okay to lock up. Maybe I was on the same wavelength as Joe.

When we got inside my apartment, I opened the windows wide. Joe stood beside me. I shivered with him that close.

"Look there's ole Davy Crockett giving us the cold shoulder." The statue of David Crockett faced away from us. He might have been looking for a bear.

"Where's the moon?"

I leaned out as far as I could. "Look over there between the trees. It's waxing toward the third quarter."

Joe rolled his eyes. "I guess that the moon is trying to say something to us."

"Sure. Why do you think it's up there?"

"Okay. Go for it."

"Well, first quarter is beginnings. Second quarter is intentions. Third is fulfillment, and full moon, well, that's just plain craziness."

"So what's this one a sign of?"

"Fulfillment. Yeah, like taking some action, stepping forward, making something happen."

I didn't look at him when I said that.

He turned me toward him, and his arms circled my back. I leaned in.

His heart was thudding like mine, and when I did look at him, he tilted my chin up and kissed me. I kissed him back.

He took a step back and tugged me closer. I followed him like a slow dance—left foot, right foot, one step, two steps, then he gently pulled me closer. I got lost somehow in the next few minutes. My heart hammered against my shirt, and I didn't know quite what to do next. Joe turned me toward the bed, and I backed up until I felt the bed pressed against the back of my knees. Gently, he lay me down. The bed creaked as we nestled there together. At last.

14

The Courthouse

The Dayton County Courthouse hovers over us here in Nuanz. I guess you didn't pay much attention if you grew up here, but the old building dominates the town. The clock tower is visible from most any point downtown and as far out as the ridge west of town. Old photos of the courthouse show folks' buggies and wagons drawn by mules on the rutted road. The First Monday crowd photos show shoulder-to-shoulder farmers, gents, and traders with their bucking horses and cows for sale and the old courthouse looming behind.

When I step out of the post office or the laundromat or walk back from the baseball field, I search for that old courthouse like an anchor to life. The best view is coming down College Street. When you get to the old Methodist manse and ease around that slightest of curves, she appears there in front of you, filling the whole end of the street from the corner drugstore to the Ben Franklin Five and Dime. She is a grand dame, and she pulls you toward her like a magnet. Her vibrations send out a call: "Come on down. I am here, and I am not going anywhere."

The red and brown brick building rises from a deep, full basement to two stories with huge windows and tall peaks on the four corners. The lights around the square were ordered special from New York and were electrified before many houses had electricity.

The three entrances with their wide porches and marble floors have sheltered groups of people as bankers and lawyers auctioned off their bankrupt property.

I have watched the deputies march the inmates up the stairs in their pinstripe uniforms from the Dayton County Jail. Some are usually chained together, and their chains jingle as they climb up the stairs and disappear inside.

The huge courtroom in the back that seats 200 people is where arraignments, trials, and county court meetings are held. Mostly older white men preside there.

There also have been big political rallies and revivals on the front lawn in past years, according to our historian, Mr. Culp. He's the local history teacher and a regular customer of mine. He always has a few things to say if anyone will listen.

Everybody in the county must make their way to the courthouse sometime during their lifetime, whether it's to vote, pay taxes, register a car, obtain a wedding license, serve jury duty, or even appear before the judge. The life of the county is there. The courthouse hovers over us and our tiny, daily acts of living.

The courthouse building was a grand accomplishment when it was finished in 1901, and it looks grand, still in pristine shape after all those years. The clock tower peers at me and perhaps keeps Nuanz's secrets to herself. She watches us and preserves our sanity when we humans teeter on the edge. In a world that is filled with injustice and meanness, she beckons us. We usually oblige. For over sixty years, she has been the center of the town and many of the people's hearts.

The biggest crowd I had seen at the courthouse was at the Christmas drawing. Local merchants gave out tickets for every dollar spent in their business from September till December. Every Saturday in December, there was a drawing on the court square. The town was covered. Mr. Jonas had donated one of the old theater spotlights, and they had hauled it up on the bank's roof. Hollywood came to town when they turned the light on and flashed it over the courthouse clock tower. You could feel the excitement rising. People had sacks and cigar boxes full of their tickets arranged in countless different ways. Rolls and rolls of tickets protruded from paper bags and stuffed pockets. Some listed their numbers on long sheets of paper or cardboard. Tickets would be drawn, and murmurs could be heard as people ran their fingers down the rows, looking for the number. This big deal ended with a drawing of $1,000 on the last Saturday before Christmas.

But most never gave a thought to the courthouse. Riding around the square was a rite of initiation for teenage drivers and a brief respite for the bored housewife. Driving around backward was a dare issued in the dead of night and executed by both young daredevils and inebriated older citizens. We knew the afternoon that Speedy Harris drove around three times the wrong way that she had experienced another stroke. But no one was brave enough to try and stop her. We simply got out of her way.

The fountain on the west side of the square was donated by the Friedman family. It was a beautiful carved fountain with water falling three different levels to the pool.

Spring officially arrived when the Whittakers slipped by watchful eyes and began their foot-washing in the fountain. They might succeed if they didn't always end up squabbling as to who went first and then slinging their winter-crusted socks at each other. Deputy Powell would be called and shoo them off before somebody got hurt. But many times, the poor goldfish couldn't survive the muddy water.

Funny how a place can speak to you. I never felt that kinship with anything in Wicket, where I was raised. Maybe I was too young and didn't pay enough attention. But Wicket had an air about it—of not giving a rat's ass about you if you lived in a rundown house or wore hand-me-down clothes. I knew what it felt like to be on the receiving end of those looks. When I came to Nuanz, I felt something different. Maybe that freed me to be myself. The world then was breaking up all around us with sit-ins and the cruel things people were doing to other human beings. I never even knew any black people till I came to Tennessee. They were over there in their own neighborhoods, churches, eating places, and I was in mine. When things around me changed, who would have ever thought I would be in the middle of it?

I learned quickly that I liked the independence I found here in Nuanz. I wanted to learn more about me and about the world I was in.

That big ole courthouse hovered over us here in Nuanz. It gave me a feeling of belonging to something bigger than myself—of counting for something. When I was next door at my window, or all the way out by the cemetery, I could feel a little shiver when I saw the top of her peeping over the buildings and trees. She, too, was all alone but planted deep in her place, implacable and immovable.

15

Joe's Last Night

It was Joe's last night in Nuanz. His riverboat tour would begin the next day, and he would be gone longer this time—two months. It worked out well that he would be gone during the big Fourth of July weekend because I sure would be busy. But when he asked me if I would still be here when he got back, I rolled my eyes. I hoped he couldn't hear the wistfulness in my voice. Every time I got used to having him around, he left. Before, I was always glad to have a little breathing room for a few days. Then I got to thinking about his eventual return.

Joe was to come around six. We were headed to Jackson for a nice meal. I dressed slowly and kept the window open to hear his car pull up. Once the square cleared, I decided to lock up and wait on the street. Common,

I know, but I didn't care. The two wooden chairs had been pulled down in front of the law office, and I dragged one back to the double doors of the Friedman Building leading upstairs. As I sat, a quietness settled around the square. No one seemed to be working late. The upstairs light at the Hays apartment was lit. Mr. Harwood's office was dark.

Suddenly, a black sedan pulled up at the front of the courthouse. I didn't recognize the car, but several people were inside. I heard voices low and rumbling. I couldn't imagine what they were doing there.

Then a tall, skinny guy climbed out of the back seat and walked over to the Confederate statue. I sat there with my arms folded. He hadn't looked my way. He seemed to be reading something on the base of the statue. Then he bent over and seemed to move something, reaching for his back pocket at the same time. What the heck was he up to? He reached up as high as he could and laid something on the corner. The car rolled down closer. He never looked around. Then he walked to the car and climbed into the back seat. They headed east and didn't even circle the square.

I stood, ready to see if the man had left something, and then Joe pulled over. I picked up my purse and climbed in beside him.

"Hey, are you ready to go?" Joe was spiffed up tonight, his hair still wet from his shower.

I slid into the car and set my purse in the floorboard. "Yeah, I am starved."

"Me, too."

Joe laughed. I could smell his aftershave. My God, I was losing my mind over him.

As we headed down College Street, I remembered the statue.

"Remind me when we get back to check something out."

"What?"

"I thought somebody left something on the rebel statue."

He rolled his eyes. "What, a joint?"

"Who knows?"

"It will probably be gone when we get back anyway."

I didn't think about the statue again. We had too much to do that last night together. I didn't want to stick my nose into somebody else's business—for a change.

Jackson is a big city by my standards. There are a lot of nice restaurants, stores, and parks there. This was where the lunch counter sit-ins and bus protests were a couple of years ago, when I got caught right in the middle. But that's also where I hooked up with Queenie.

Joe and I talked so easily about things. We were there in the big city with all the lights and people before I realized it. He parked, and we strolled up and down the downtown blocks for a while. Finally, we grabbed a table outside on the sidewalk, and Joe ordered us a pizza. It was nice to sit and watch the people and think maybe you were halfway grown.

After dark, we started back to Nuanz. I scooted over next to him as he drove. The radio was playing the top forty. Here I was riding next to a boy that I had gone all the way with and thinking about going there again. I wondered what my daddy would have thought of Joe. Not that it mattered, but I like to think he would have liked Joe.

"Joe, what do you do on that boat every night?"

"What do you mean? I eat, I sleep, I work the lines when it's my turn."

"No, I know that. What do you do at night after all the work's done? Do you talk to the other guys?"

"Sometimes we talk. We listen to the radio. Some guys read or even work on stuff. There's this one guy that's got a knack for carving. He brings wood with him to whittle on and make little pieces of stuff."

"Like what?"

"You know—animals, rabbits, squirrels, or old fat women with boobs, grouchy men with pipes in their mouths."

I laughed. "What do you do?"

"Oh, different things. I like to watch the water. Think about where we are headed. Look at the lights on the banks." He paused. "Of course, look at the stars."

"Oh, so you are into that stargazing stuff?" I couldn't help but grin.

"Well, I used to know this girl that was eat up with it all. She could name stars and constellations and talk all kinds of nonsense."

"She sounds pretty smart to me."

"She thinks she is."

I hit his shoulder, and he groaned. "Ouch, be careful. I'm driving."

"So, it's kind of neat being out there, I guess."

"Yes, it is. If everything's calm like now when the weather's good, it gives me a chance to think."

"About what?"

"You know, stuff."

"What stuff?"

"Important stuff like what I'm gonna eat for breakfast, and if I have any clean underwear before we get to Vicksburg."

I made as if I was gonna scoot over to my door.

"Hey, wait a minute now." Joe let go of the steering wheel and grabbed for me.

I pretended to try and slap his hand away.

"No, really, what do you think about?"

"At night, when there's no one around but the wind and the stars and the moon if it's shining, I think about what is out there. I think about what I want to do—all the people that I know—the ones I don't want to ever see again and the ones I want to see more of."

"Which one am I?"

He took his eyes off the road and looked at me. "Mesha, you know."

Then it was quiet except for the song playing, and I felt so happy and lucky. Damn lucky, and that was really all I needed right now.

16

Edna's Favors and the Power of the Moon

Edna was not known as a vengeful person, but she did keep score. She called it an accounting. She carried most information in her head, I reckon, of who owed her what and when. She always knew, and she always collected.

Many times, she didn't deal just in cash, either. Those debts could be a slight pressure to be quiet, stop complaining, or a "favor," as she liked to call them. "Hon, do me a favor" was an often-heard phrase, followed by a suggestion that might become a directive. When someone had the guts to say no to her, I have heard her say, "Hon, let's act like you didn't say that out loud."

Edna did her good deeds in secret. I imagine those secrets she held close to her heart were the ones we will never know. Her bad deeds were in the mix, too. Rest assured, Edna was no angel. Everyone has their limits. She could work a room and a tight-fisted, cranky old man as easily as an evangelist at a summer tent meeting. Many times, she left passing the plate to her sidekicks—Johnny or Moose.

Every once in a while, I asked her if she was writing in her little book of Edna's secrets. One time, she whipped the book out of her overflowing bra and waved it at me. "See, I keep it here close," she said, laughing all the while.

Another time, she opened her book of secrets and began reading a portion to me. Something like: "Tell M. about how to know if he's lying or just making it up as he goes along."

She raised her eyebrows at me. She turned a page and ran her finger down. Then she read, "Remember to bury those bodies extra deep."

"Go on," I said.

Then she laughed and said, "You are gonna have to wait until I'm gone, hon."

God, I love that Edna Love.

Then her days away from us became a normal thing. At first, when she arrived, she was usually purring like a well-fed cat. Her signature scent—Fleurs de Rocaille Jardin—floated in her space as she moved. The earrings dangled and those chopstick antennae gleamed in the overhead lights of the Bluebird Cafe. I tried to get her to 'fess up, but she would turn the conversation around immediately without saying to me, "That's none of your business."

Once those things settled down, I got all goofy-headed over that sex thing I had going on with Joe. Damn. I didn't know sometimes what on earth I was doing. I would get all revved just thinking about him, then try to slow it down, knowing I really didn't want to slow it down.

Honestly, Mesha, why do you want to make yourself miserable? I thought. Can't you let well enough alone? There's plenty of folks out there to make you miserable without you even trying.

So I tried to pace myself.

But the moon was no help at all. When the heart is involved, you can always blame it on the moon. She is powerful all by herself. In fact, her nearness keeps our planet in its perpetual tilt. Without the moon, we would just topple over.

That's another reason I always kept my eye on what phase the moon was in when things were going on down here. We were nearing the full moon, and that was always a time for all-out craziness. We had our share of crazies here in Nuanz. I was watchful.

Auction Prep

Mr. S was having a big auction on the weekend of the Fourth of July. This year, July Fourth was on a Monday, so people started celebrating on the Thursday before. There would be two quick auctions on Friday with the big finale on Saturday. The auction house had been unloading vans and tractor trailers for over ten days. Mr. S had hired extra hands to move and unbox, and Grace had gotten some extra hours to help inventory.

I must admit that Grace was ambitious to be only thirteen years old, but she's one of those kids with an old soul. I was glad I had helped her get in with Mr. S. She liked all the stuff, and she was getting better at socializing.

Like me, she tended to go it alone. I hoped she would figure out how to get along with more people. But she covered her tender heart and protected herself.

Edna and I went by Monday afternoon the week before the auction to see if there was anything we could do. Mr. S is always open to seeing Edna. I left Louise in charge of the Liars' Table hangers-on at the cafe. There were three old dudes who were widowed and didn't want to go home to fix a bacon sandwich for supper alone. Edna and I rode in her Cadillac to the auction house.

Six guys were unloading a truck. Some walked boxes to the open door; others used dollies to roll the boxes into the back of the building. The men had their sleeves rolled up, and bandanas caught the sweat from their heads. Although there was plenty of shade, the humidity was bearing down. You could tell who was really in charge—the ones with a clipboard. At least they knew what direction to send the boxes. Just as we got there, another truck pulled in, and the driver unfastened the doors and pulled out a ramp.

Now that we knew what a big deal it was when the trucks rolled in with auction items, we were excited to watch. I had already ordered double my usual holiday groceries for the cafe, and I thought maybe I hadn't ordered enough.

We went inside the kitchen, and there sat Grace and Lucy on each end of the big kitchen table. Clipboards and papers were piled everywhere, and Grace was matching numbers on the lists with numbers on the boxes. She hadn't seen us, but Edna and I both grinned as we watched her. Grace held her mouth in a grim line with her head bent low over the papers. Her skinny arms poked out of her shirt, and her hair was held back in a ponytail streaming down her back. There was nothing shy about her now.

One of the colored guys came from the back and said, "Miss Gracie, we're ready to open some more boxes." She nodded her head and reached for another clipboard and a big red pen. She stood and saw us.

"Hi, Squirt, are you in charge here?" I asked.

She laughed, then ducked her head. "Not yet. What do you want?"

"Nothing. We're here to see if you've got everything organized."

She held the papers and shrugged. "Working on it, I guess."

She turned then and followed the guy down the dark hallway.

Lucy ran the adding machine as she sorted through an invoice stack. We spoke, and she nodded her head, her lips moving as if she was counting. We wandered the other way toward Mr. S's office. As usual, he was on the phone but waved us inside.

I sank into a low, velveteen, antique chair. Edna sat on the love seat and kept her eyes on Guido. I tried to decide what that thing was behind his head on the wall. Some kind of stuffed animal? Not anything from around here.

Mr. S hung up the phone and eased back into his chair, rocking it back and forth with a clicking sound. He smiled. "Well, good afternoon, ladies. How are things with you guys?"

I loved his accent. It sounded like something you'd hear on one of those gangster movies.

I was always intrigued with the gold ring on his left hand. It was not a wedding band, more like a signet ring with a huge red stone sitting high and carving all around. I wondered if he ever took off the ring. I wondered, too, if he had ever hit anybody with it. Split somebody's lip or blackened somebody's eye, maybe?

"Mesha."

I drew my eyes away from the ring.

"Mesha, did you bring me some pie?"

I grinned. "I wanted to, but Edna was in too big of a hurry."

He laughed, as did Edna.

"Are you ready for your big shindig?" Edna touched the back of her upswept French twist as she smiled at him.

"I hope we'll be ready in time."

"How many people are you expecting? Must be a lot from the looks of all the stuff you're bringing in."

He handed us each a flier, an extra-long sheet with red and blue words shrieking the news: "House of Guido Salvatorre presents: American Classics Celebrate the 4th of July." There were eagles and flags flying all over the circular and so many items listed that the words all blended together. Glassware, antique lamps, bedroom suites, fine china, silver, coins, lamps, cherry, mahogany, oak. Then names I had no idea who or what they were: Stickley, Mission, chifforobes, claw-footed, teasers, parlor sets. Then a list of estates with names that were as foreign as Mr. S.

"Whew. This looks like a goat roping." Edna's eyes were dancing. "I may need to order a few more kegs for the Oasis." We all laughed.

"Do you need any help?" I hesitated to offer, hoping he would say everything was handled.

He smiled politely and said, "No, dear Mesha, we have everything under control. But I hope you'll come by. I am expecting another Bugatti in tomorrow's shipment."

"Really? What is it this time?"

"Oh, you'll have to wait and see."

"What if it's gone before I get here?"

"I think this one may have my name on it already."

He steepled his brown fingers together, his eyes dancing with a light in them.

"I want to see that then."

I really did. Since I had found out more about this Bugatti guy, I liked seeing his work. Who would have thought a little girl from Wicket, Mississippi, would ever know about Rembrandt Bugatti, much less see some of his work?

"What time does everything start?"

"The crowds start gathering Thursday. Anywhere from morning on. They can look, but they cannot buy. Friday, we begin at noon and start with small items until five o'clock. Then after supper, we're going to have an outside-only auction with some big items. We're stringing lights all over the parking lot. Saturday begins at ten and ends at seven. Then I am closing for the month."

18

Warning Bells

On my day off this week before the weekend bash, I finished my laundry and strolled over to Salvatorre's. I wanted to see if the Bugatti had come in before the big auction.

Gracie wasn't there today. Lucy, the older lady who worked for Mr. S, opened the door.

"We're not open until Thursday. Oh, it's you," she said, and stood there in the doorway.

"Is Mr. S busy?"

She stood there for a minute with her hand on the door as she contemplated whether to let me in.

"He will probably want to see you for a few."

She stood back and reluctantly opened the door wider.

"Thanks," I muttered as I skulked down the entrance hall as if I were a criminal.

"Go on back. He's probably on the phone."

The back part of the auction house still looked like somebody's home. The thick carpeting muffled any footsteps. The lights were always dim. This house had a smell, like most do. Not unpleasant but not cheery, either. Maybe there was a lingering whiff of the chloroform from the undertaking side, probably soaked into the rafters and boards. There was a bit of mothballs and staleness, too, as if no fresh air had been allowed to enter. Not scary but not welcoming, at least not to me.

I walked down the hall silently, and I could hear Mr. S's voice but could not make out any words. When I stopped at the door, he had his back turned to me. He rocked gently back and forth as though in time to some beat playing in his head. He was speaking in a foreign language softly but urgently. He talked as he rocked, and then he would stop when the other voice took over.

I knocked on the door softly, and Mr. S never turned around. Then, afraid I would hear something I wasn't supposed to, I knocked a little louder. He turned, startled at first. For a second, I saw a coldness—maybe anger there.

Then he smiled and motioned for me to come in. He turned the chair around and shifted the phone to his right ear, grabbed his pen, and wrote something. He spoke rapidly again—words I didn't understand—and quickly hung up the phone. He broke out in a smile that I couldn't quite believe. *What made you smile like that?* I thought.

"Mesha. Come, come. How are you, my cherie?"

I couldn't help myself. I smiled back. "Oh, I am fine. This is my day off. I wanted to see if the shipment was in."

"Yes, yes. Come with me. It's back here." He touched my arm as he held the door open for me, and we walked back to the chapel.

"I have a couple of things you will want to see."

We walked to the walnut buffet with the locked doors, and he touched something on the side that made them spring open. There were several boxes and cloth-wrapped pieces. He pulled out a little ballerina statue.

She was standing on one toe with the other leg bent underneath her skirt. She was faded with a chip on her standing leg.

"See," he said, pointing to the chip. "This decreases the price and value some but not too much."

"What is it?" I said.

"An early work of Degas. He loved the ballet and young girls. Maybe too much."

I didn't say anything. But the expression on the girl's face was studied and quiet.

"Do you like it?"

"I suppose if you like ballet dancing. I haven't even seen a real ballerina in person."

Mr. S wrapped the ballerina statue and put her back on the shelf.

"This is what I really wanted to show you."

He moved a couple of boxes and then brought a wooden box to the front. He turned and found a place on the table behind us.

He took a pocketknife from his pants pocket and pried open the lid. He pulled out the straw and layers of gray padding; then he placed a big lump on the table with a thud. I could feel his eyes on me as he began to unwrap the object. Then I began to see what it was.

"Is it another Bugatti?"

He nodded.

"Is it the one you've been looking for?"

"Not quite. But it's a beauty."

He pulled out a bronze hippo. I laughed aloud. He joined me. The light shone on its dark polished skin.

"Look at its ears—they're so tiny." I started to reach out to touch them and then realized I shouldn't.

"Go ahead. It's all right."

I touched the ears and ran my fingers down the wide snout. The metal was so smooth, like velvet.

"Poor little hippo. Why did he sculpt a hippo? They were under water when I tried to see one at the zoo. Edna took me a while back."

"They can be very shy and also very protective of their young."

I couldn't take my eyes off the mother hippo.

"Bugatti was like that—shy. He felt more at ease around animals than people. That's why he studied them there at the zoo in Austria," Mr. S explained.

"Maybe he felt a kinship with them. Locked in their cages. Looking out but never free."

Mr. S lifted the hippo closer for another look. "I don't know."

"Well, I love this little hippo. Are you going to sell it?"

"I haven't decided yet. I might keep it for a while until I find the tiger."

"Oh, what tiger is that?"

"There are many Bugatti cats. Tigers, leopards, lions. There's something about the cat sculptures that are intriguing."

I nodded.

"Cats have a certain power and cunning, beautiful and deadly at the same time. Hmmm?"

Mr. S's eyes glinted like the ring on his finger.

"I am waiting now for one. My patience is wearing thin. It should have been here already."

He set the hippo down, and I reached out to touch the sculpture once more.

"You know the poem, how does it go? 'Tyger, Tyger burning bright.'" He waited. Then my lips moved as he said the next line. " 'In the forests of the night.'"

I glanced at Mr. S, who stared at me with a strange expression. I was mesmerized by his voice.

" 'What immortal hand or eye can frame its fearful symmetry.'"

Then he laughed and placed his hand on the hippo's tail.

"Hippo, the river horse. Where is your mate? What is your call? Are you ready to ride the river and sink into the mud forever?"

I shivered for some reason. Then the moment was over. I came back to now—standing here in this mortuary chapel with a slick-looking foreigner—and wondered, "Hey, girl, is something going on you don't know about?"

Mr. S put the hippo back in its crate. We wandered through the aisles. He pulled out a pink perfume bottle with a tall, cut-glass stopper in it. "Do you think Edna would like this?"

"Oh, who knows what Edna will like? Believe me, she will tell you." We laughed.

"How is Miz Edna? I have not seen her lately."

I looked at him sideways. Was he nosing around? That was out of character for him. I played it straight.

"I haven't seen her much lately, either. She must be busy with some world-changing deal somewhere."

He nodded his head. "You never know with Edna."

"Well, I better get going. Thanks for the visit, Mr. S."

"Come by anytime, Mesha. You know you are always welcome."

"Your next cup of coffee at the Bluebird will be freshly made. I promise."

As the heavy front door closed, I walked down the steps and felt a little chill creep across the back of my neck, like someone was watching me. Then I crossed the street and took my time walking in the sunshine back to my apartment on the court square.

PART III
THE DEED

Paradise Alley

There is a section of colored town called East Side with certain places where white people are not welcomed. Early black families made their homes there, and black-owned businesses are scattered throughout. One street named Paradise Alley runs south from the river for four blocks. No one knew exactly why it was called Paradise Alley. What a name, right?

One afternoon on my day off, I was down at Rem's Place with Queen and Miss Florence, Rem's sister. I had finished my greens and cornbread, rested my forearms on the counter, and lifted my iced tea glass to my lips for that last cold sip. The usual sounds floated in the air after the dinnertime rush at Rem's. A few deep rumbles came from some men in the far corner finishing their lunches. Boy Blue and Sun Man racked the pool balls for a game.

I felt the breeze from the door as it opened and then heard the door slam shut. Suddenly, everyone grew quiet. I set my tea glass down and peeked into the mirror to see if I could figure out who it was. She walked by me, bent over a bit, with a turban wrapped around her head and her arms full of a canvas bag. Rem looked in the kitchen doorway for his sister, who had disappeared there.

Madam Evaline Taliafarro stood next to me and waited.

Rem said, "Madam, how you doing?"

When she nodded her head, her glasses slipped down farther on her nose. There was a bell-like tinkling. I caught a sweet but medicinal sniff of something I could not name. As I turned to acknowledge her, she shifted the canvas bag to the stool beside me. She was tall, thin, and very dark. When she turned to look at me, her eyes were the greenest green I had ever seen. She wore long, jangled earrings made of delicate silver filigree with quarter moons and stars. They tinkled against each other. Her gaze jumped over me when I dared to say her name, "Madam," and then she turned and walked to the end of the counter, waiting with hands on her hips.

Then everyone began talking again. The billiard balls clacked against each other. Rem dried off his hands and walked back to the kitchen to summon his sister to deal with Madam.

I sat there as still as the country mouse that I am, but I couldn't hear what she said to Florence. They talked too low. Then they both walked into the kitchen, and even though I stalled as much as I could, I had to leave before she came out.

Since that horrible summer when Noah Johnson was drowned, I learned more about the black community in Nuanz. Some from Queen and Miss Florence. Some from keeping my white mouth shut and listening.

Madam Evaline was a witch, they said. She came from Louisiana and was John Taliafarro's second wife. Queen had told me about her one day when we walked past her house. She lived on the riverside block of Paradise Alley. That section began as the closely guarded black community after the Civil War. Paradise Alley hosted both the higher echelon of black society and a nice mixture of ordinary middle-class folks, too. Doctors, midwives, revered teachers, and preachers lived there or nearby. There were also working-class families—beauticians, barbers, field hands, grocery store owners, morticians, and farm hands. Many had lived here for generations. Some bore the name of their slave owners. Some had grown up on nearby farms or had stayed close to relatives here. You could try to figure out who was kin, but it wasn't easy. The best thing to do was be careful what you said if you didn't know for sure.

The home place of the Taliafarro family was a large, white, frame house in the center of Paradise Alley with a wraparound porch and French grilled railing. The sycamore trees shaded garden parties in the late summer evenings. The honeysuckle vines on the back lot welcomed young courting couples with a sweet scent. On the lower end next to the river was the two-story, yellow, frame, rambling house that some say might be the source of the street's original name. Whether that paradise was a physical or spiritual space, no one knew for sure now.

The mainstay of the community was the Taliafarro family. *Taliafarro* is Italian for "iron worker." The first black male to bear that name was Moses "Noc" Taliafarro. He was a blacksmith by trade, said to be strong in body and presence. He was in charge of laying out the streets when the town began. The plat was drawn, and Moses was soon put in charge of building the roads. He could work at night by a kerosene lantern, mark the lines, and keep the crews working. Besides his physical strength, he possessed this incredible night vision, which surpassed any ordinary man's ability to see at night. Like some night creature, he could see what lay ahead in the darkness even on moonless nights. All the Taliafarros do night work. They're the best at this. That's where the nickname came from—*Noc* for "nocturnal."

The other talent that some Taliafarros had was a supernatural one. At least one in each generation had an ability to see visions, halos, and other sightings. Most people just whispered about this talent. But John T. was known to have this second sight, too. That's why he was a living legend there on Paradise Alley.

From that early work, Moses Taliafarro bought his freedom and a large tract of land on the edge of the woods that led to the swamp and down to the riverbank of the little North Fork.

He left the land to his firstborn son. His grandson Noc bought more land when he could. Their rental properties were a source of pride for many black families to live in.

Some say the name Paradise Alley described how it felt living there—protected and safe. Heaven on earth. Some say the alley's name kept it real and honest. People may have tried to tread the streets of gold, but their shoes kept scuffing grit.

Even Rem told me one day, "All is not perfect here. But if we can stay upright even when the moon pulls us, that hope is what keeps Paradise Alley alive."

No one knows for sure what Paradise Alley was meant to be, except a home and a haven to many black citizens of this town.

Florence told me one day, "Paradise Alley protects us. You breathe easier there. Most of us see both sides. There's good and evil everywhere. You know if you are honest with yourself," she paused, lifting one hand to the right and another to the left, "you can reach out and feel them both."

"Everybody has their share of darkness, but if a pinpoint of light flickers, you gotta fan the flames," she smiled, dropping her left hand but slightly waving her right one. "Always in moderation, Mesha."

The first four blocks of that land stayed in the Taliafarro family for all these years. Madam, John Taliafarro's wife, lived in the house there close to the river. John got on a train and went to New Orleans after his first wife died. He came back with Madam. They had three daughters and two sons. Her auntie and a cousin lived there with Madam now. She raised a garden, bartered her vegetables for goods, and raised her own goats. But everyone knew if you needed something charmed off, or curative powders, or out-and-out hoo-doo, she was the woman to see.

After the Taliafarro daughters married and moved off, Madam isolated herself. People knew to tread lightly around Madam, but they respected her, too. Noc stayed uptown in the family home on Paradise Alley. Madam had her strengths, and Noc had his. I learned all this in bits and pieces from my time spent at Rem's Place.

20

Mesha and Queen on Top of the World

On my own without Joe for weeks, I spent as much time as I could with the rest of my gang: Queen, Edna, and Grace. Since Edna was gone so much now, I concentrated more on Queen and Grace. Some days, we hung out at Rem's. Some days, Queen came to see me after work. Grace appeared at the cafe or my apartment from time to time.

Queen's love life was way ahead of mine. She kept at least three different guys vying for her attention. She loved dangling her men in her life, but like me, she needed some girl time. I heard there was something going on that weekend on East Side and asked if I could go with her.

"Girl, we don't have white people down at Rem's on the weekends, you know that."

"Well, I think Rem wouldn't mind."

"He might not say anything, but he would mind. You want me to go down to the Oasis with you?"

"Sure." I knew she was kidding.

"Maybe when I am blind drunk, I might ride by real fast."

"Come on, it's not that bad."

But we both knew it was.

"Come hang out with me for a while before you start the big party night," I said.

She agreed to climb on the roof with me. When I got off work, I fixed us a jar full of lemonade with a spike of gin.

We climbed the fire escape just as it was starting to get dark. The moon was rising in the east, and I felt good being here above the world.

"What lucky guy is taking you out tonight?" I asked.

"Hmm. That would be Isaiah."

"Who's that?"

"He's one of Big Noc's grandsons."

"Now who is Noc again?"

"I told you 'bout Noc Taliafarro. He's the mayor of East Side."

"Oh, yeah. He's married to Madam Evaline?"

"Sort of. They kind of drifted apart."

"Tell me again why y'all call him Noc?"

"His real name is John Moses Taliafarro, but every firstborn in his family is called Noc. It stands for nocturnal—you know, night."

"What's the night thing again?"

"They say it's something about their eyes. If you notice, he's got big eyes, and from the family genes, he can see things better than anybody at night."

"That's weird. Like an owl or something."

"Yeah. But the old people say it was a charm thing that his great-grandfather got. He was born under some kind of eclipsing moon or something. You know how those tales go."

We each took a sip of our drinks. Twilight settled over the town, and the moon began its arc over the courthouse trees.

"You probably haven't ever heard about anything like that."

"My grandmother knew a lot about charms and old-timey ways," I said. "She used to talk about stuff like that."

"I don't believe all of it, but sometimes there's stuff you can't really explain."

"Yes, that's right."

We sat for a minute. Queen rattled the ice in her glass, and I poured her more gin and lemonade.

I thought about my granny and my home down in Wicket. I hadn't thought of the signs she used to tell me about in a long time.

"Noc don't say much, but when he does, everybody listens."

"I bet."

"We don't know exactly how old he is, but he don't move like an old man at all. They say that's because he's got the sight. You know that Taliafarro sight. He knows when evil is about. Sometime, he handles it. Sometime, he ignores it."

Queen took another long sip of her drink. "When something happens with the black folks and the law needs some help, they usually go to Noc. He knows how to handle the white people. Those that have any sense, that is."

"Well, they are few and far between."

"Why do you want to know so much about us black people?"

"I don't know. When I moved here and met Grace and Noah, and all that sit-in business was going on, that got to me."

"Yeah, that was intense."

"Then when old Edd Biggs murdered Noah, that slammed me hard. Still does."

"You need to be careful. All black people are not like me. Cozying up with some white girl from Mississippi. They don't trust you because you are white."

"I know. I know. I am careful."

We sat for a few minutes more. Then she said, "If you ain't got any more joy juice, I better get going."

I laughed. "Go on and have fun. I will just sit here by myself and wait for the booger bear to come get me."

"Girl, he wouldn't have you for long."

Queen climbed down the fire escape. I heard her footsteps across the wooden floor and down the steps below me.

The stars were coming out now, one by one. There was going to be a nearly full moon. Back west, I couldn't see any fires yet or anything going on out there. Then I heard a freight train coming far off; its whistle sounded like a strange, lonely bird. Like me.

I decided I better get down off this roof before I saw something I shouldn't.

I climbed down and started across the upstairs floor. Suddenly, I saw a light shine through the street-door window. I waited a minute. Then the door slowly creaked open. I stood back in the corner, hoping whoever it was couldn't see me. I didn't recognize the man standing there.

I looked around to see if there was anywhere I could hide or anything I could use to defend myself. All I had in my hands were the empty fruit jar and two crumpled paper cups. I tried not to breathe.

The man stared at the directory on the wall, which said nothing at all about me. When he glanced up the stairs, I couldn't make out his face in the dim light. Then he put his foot on the first step. I tried Dr. Huffman's office door. It was locked, but at least I would be out of sight if the man climbed the stairs. I didn't think I could sneak across the floor to my apartment, though. The stairs creaked again as he came up a few more steps. I squatted down as close to the floor as I could get in the dark. My heart was jumping. I was backed into a corner against an enemy I didn't know.

Should I stand and shout at him? I took a deep breath and was ready to leap when the courthouse clock started striking. He jumped, startled, and then bolted down the steps and out the door. I counted to twenty as slowly as I could. I thought I heard him running down the street, but it could have been my imagination.

I walked as quickly and quietly as I could to my apartment, shut the door, and locked it. I took a deep breath. *You are safe, Mesha*, I thought.

I went to the window and peeked out on the square. No one was there. Nothing moved except an old truck around the far side of the square. Then I heard a sudden swoosh as a night creature darted through the treetops.

I waited a few minutes, then grabbed my baseball bat, ran down the stairs, and locked the outside doors. I needed to be more careful. What on earth was that man doing snooping around here after hours?

Sometimes being a brave young woman in Nuanz, Tennessee, is hard.

21

Solitary

Being alone can be good. A solitary existence is not that bad. Oh, I get bored with crazy ole me thinking my dark thoughts, wandering over the past and hanging my hopes on a distant future. But I guess being who I am is okay. I came from nothing, but I never felt cheated.

Being alone helps me figure things out. People think I am standoffish, but I guess my aloneness is like a protection against folks getting too close, asking too many questions. I know the longer I hold on to my solitariness, the harder it will be to tolerate others. That can't be too good for me—never mind how I've shortchanged the world out of getting to know Meshac Brownlow.

The first rhyme I remember my granny repeating to me was the rhyme about the moon. I think that we must have been outside looking at the sky.

"I see the moon. The moon sees me," she'd say and then wait.

I would say, "God bless the moon and God bless me."

I still say that when I gaze upward. It's like breathing—a natural part of me. I have always felt the moon, absent during the dark phase and present, pulling strongly, during its fullness.

Just think, when I stand and look up at the moon, no matter my circumstances, that same moon is in everybody's sky. Irene, Roy, and Aunt Flo. Joe on the boat or Queen driving her car in the cool night air. Grace with her newfound friends and her tough shell of resilience. Edna Love with her hand on her hip watching. Even Lawyer Malone's dog on his nightly rounds checking the neighbors' cats, listening for a voice or a pat on his head, waiting. We wait and we eventually look up. Each one has a different thought but the same heart buried underneath days of delight and nights of dread.

It's funny how when you're in the middle of something, you can't really see the big picture. You never think about the effect of taking that one path that never leads back. Most of our lives are filled with ordinary living. I call it day-by-day living. You don't plan too far ahead, don't buy too many lottery tickets, but you do stamp white horses (my granny's phrase that means wishing for luck) and listen for that word from beyond while the universe is holding its breath. You may stumble over the edge or lift your head and find the light. Me? I don't even know for sure what I'm looking for, but I'll know when I see it.

Sometimes I just want to sit with my back against the courthouse door and smoke a cigarette—if I knew how. Then lean back in a full tilt, squint my eyes, and gaze as far as I can down College Street and say, "Come and get me if you think you can."

22

Grace, Meshac, and the Moon

"Look up. Just look up," I told Grace.

She rolled her eyes at me, then tilted her head back. Big, bored sigh. "What? What am I supposed to see?"

"I don't know. You tell me."

She shifted to her other bored side, then looked again.

"I don't know. Clouds, blue sky. Is that a jet?"

I gazed at the sky, too. "Yep. See its tail shooting out behind. That's called a contrail. It's like a clue. Follow this and you can guess where I'm going.

"Seeing a jet is like finding a four-leaf clover—good luck—so I always wish on them when they race across the sky."

"That's about the dumbest thing I ever heard," Grace said. "It's an airplane carrying some people somewhere. Not a rare thing. Not even remotely magical. Why would you wish on something like that?"

"I don't know. I started doing it when I was a kid. There weren't any stars to wish on in the middle of the day, so I always watched for a jet and wished on it. Sometimes there'd be three or four over the place."

She shook her head like a forty-year-old. "Mesha, you are so weird sometimes."

"Yes, I am. And I am proud of it. Come inside, and I will fix you a Coke. No charge."

We settled into my apartment. The windows were open, but hot air drifted in. Grace draped herself on the window's ledge and stared at the court square.

"Don't you love it here in your apartment?"

"Yes, I do."

"This place beats that dreary old Nuanz Motor Inn."

"Yep. How are things at the Aunt Virginia Hotel? Are you helping her out?"

"Of course. If I want to live."

"Poor baby." I reached out to pat her head, and she turned away.

"Stop that. I'm grown—head patting isn't funny anymore."

"What's going on, Grace?"

"I don't know if I should talk to you."

"That's a clear sign that you should talk to me."

She blushed. "I don't know how to tell you."

I gave her a minute. "You can say anything to me. You know you saved my life not so long ago." Then I waited.

I reached over and turned on the fan. Under the blades' slow rotation, last night's newspaper ruffled and skated over the surface of the bed, then lay back down.

I tried not to say anything. But the longer the silence lingered, the more nervous I got, and it mushroomed into a cold, dark feeling. Grace drew her knees to her chest and gazed at the court square again. I was about to tell her to never mind when she turned and let her legs dangle to the floor.

"It's Mr. S."

My mother radar spiraled out of my head. *Stay calm, Mesha.*

"What about Mr. S?"

"I don't know. Sometimes he gives me the creeps."

"Yeah, how?"

"He sounds like he's really angry on the phone."

"Maybe that's just business talk."

She said something, but her voice was so low I could barely hear her. "What?" I asked.

"He stares at me sometimes. It feels weird."

I waited a few seconds. "If he makes you uncomfortable, you should quit. Money's not that important."

She gave me that stubborn look she gets sometimes. "No, I am not a quitter. Something else is going on, I think."

"Like what? Has he said anything to you? You know, out of the way?"

"No, not really. But something's not right."

I tried to stay calm. "If you don't feel safe, you know you should get out of there, don't you?"

"Oh, it's not that. Plus, I am learning a lot about how to do business stuff. They think I am just a little teenage girl but . . ."

She lifted the magazine from the rocker and began thumbing through the pages.

"Grace, you have to promise to come straight to me if something happens. Don't wait."

She stared at me with an old soul behind her eyes that had seen things some old heads haven't ever seen. I hadn't seen that expression on her face in a long time.

"I will."

She laid the magazine in her lap. I gave her a couple of minutes.

"So do you want me to stick my big nose in your business?"

She smiled then. "Maybe. If you don't mind."

"I do mind. But I guess I owe you. That saving-my-life thing keeps hanging over my head."

She laughed and walked over to me. "Thank you," she said into my shoulder.

"Let me think about it for a few days."

"Sure. Whenever."

Here I went again, getting into somebody else's business. There must be a name for that. Meddling?

23

Skinny Stranger at the July Fourth Auction

The Fourth of July Salvatorre auction was all it claimed to be. Out-of-state cars, trucks, and flatbed trailers came rolling into Nuanz on Thursday morning. The Nuanz Motor Inn filled up within a few hours, and Thursday night dinner was full to the gills. I had to call Bill to come help Mr. Rob in the kitchen. Edna sent Moose to help us stock the walk-in. I thought maybe I had overbought, but by eight o'clock Friday evening, I was worried I didn't have enough food to get through breakfast.

I wanted to tell my regular customers to quit gawking and putting on airs so they could eat and get out. But they were like me, wanting to see what these strangers were like and why they were really here. This was the biggie that would far surpass the other auctions.

Sheriff Hensley came at noon on Friday and stood at the front door. I was trying to deliver the finished orders to the right tables. I nodded at him. He wanted to tell me something. The next circuit I made, he was still standing there.

"Hey, Sheriff, can I get you something?"

"No, I am looking for somebody."

"Who? Maybe I can help you."

His eyes kept sweeping the room. Made me kind of nervous.

"Is it one of our regulars?"

"No, there was a tall, thin man over at the auction who looked kind of familiar."

"So is he here?"

"I don't see him."

I turned back to the pickup counter, knowing I couldn't hesitate if all these folks were gonna get fed.

After the lunch crowd cleared out, I sat down to make a deposit, and Mr. Rob and Bill stood on the front sidewalk to watch the crowd.

"Leave the door open so we can clear out some of this smoke and grease," I hollered at Mr. Rob.

As I stacked the bills and started the check roll, I felt somebody in the cafe. There was a man sitting by himself so far back in the corner I could barely see him. He was hunched over the table with his forearms on the top and his head hung low. He stayed that way for a while. I had about finished counting the bills when I heard a loud *thunk*. His head lay on the table, and he wasn't moving.

"Mister, are you all right?"

He didn't answer. I thought I saw his chest move. I hated to touch him, but I tapped his shoulder. "Mister, are you all right?" I repeated.

He sat there with his greasy head on the table. His big, white hands were clenched. Nothing moved. I jiggled the table and cleared my throat and said again, "Mister, are you okay?"

Suddenly, he jerked his head and stared at me with whiskey-soaked eyes.

"Where am I? What? Where am I?"

"The Bluebird Cafe."

He didn't seem to hear me. I didn't want to get too close, but I thought I was safe.

"Are you sick or something?"

He stared past me, leaning back in his chair.

"Do you need some help or a glass of water or something?"

He started shaking then, like a shudder from his neck down through his shoulders. He wrapped his arms around his chest as if to stop the shaking. I didn't know if he was sick or scared or crazy. I backed up a step or two.

"Let me get you a glass of water."

He nodded his head and tried to lean back farther in the chair. I ran to the counter and filled two glasses with ice water. I studied his face as I brought the water to him.

"Thanks," he said, and drank an entire glass in three or four gulps. He still didn't look like his mind was clear.

"Where did you say this was?"

"This is Nuanz. This is the Bluebird Cafe. You came in for lunch, I reckon."

He nodded his head. "Where is everybody?"

I laughed but not too loudly. "They ate and left. You just sat and slept, I guess."

He didn't smile or blink.

"Are you feeling bad?" I asked.

"I don't know—kind of shaky like."

"Are you in town for the Salvatorre auction?"

He nodded. "I must have lost my way." His eyes were clouded, and his voice was rough like sandpaper.

"Yes, I think you have. Do you feel like eating?"

"No, ma'am. If you could let me sit here a few more minutes."

"Sure. I will be up front."

I went back to my deposit, and Bill and Rob wandered in. I tried to get them to notice the stranger in the back, but they were too busy complaining about how overworked they were.

Finally, I said, leaning my head toward the back, "We still have one customer."

They blinked like two old owls, and I pointed my thumb to the table. The stranger was staring out the window now.

Mr. Rob said to me, "Who is that?"

I just shrugged my shoulders.

After another half hour or so, Mr. Partee and his grandchildren came in. The kids were talking and clattering around. They ordered Cokes and pie, and when I checked later, the stranger had disappeared.

The only thing that assured me he had been there was the crumpled dollar bill he left under the empty water glasses and the clumps of dried mud under the table.

By then, the rapid patter of the auctioneer's voice peppered the quiet downtown. The heat and sun settled over us. I took the deposit to the bank and strolled back to the cafe.

I knew it would be a long night. Dinner started early, and the restaurant didn't close till nearly eleven. I didn't think of the stranger again till I stumbled up the stairs to my apartment. Once I had shed my greasy clothes and stepped out of the shower, I sat at my open window. A man walked across the square toward the Confederate statue. I couldn't be sure, but he reminded me of the sleeping stranger that afternoon. Lo and behold, if he didn't stop at the corner of the soldier and reach toward the foot where the gun butt stood. Then he lowered his arm, walked past the soldier, crossed the street, and headed toward Paradise Alley. I was too tired to even think about what it meant, if it meant anything. I fell into bed and didn't turn over till my alarm clock clanged at four in the morning.

The big day dawned for Mr. S, and everyone was raring to go. The crowds energized me. Everyone was enjoying themselves. We made it fine through a long breakfast hour. Everyone cleared out by ten o'clock when the final big sale started. Lolly had agreed to give me some relief on Saturday and come in as my backup.

Edna rolled by and parked in the alley, and we walked the two blocks to the auction. The items were going fast, and excited people were hauling off their treasures. Mr. Horace, the Popsicle man, jogged back and forth from his cart to Hays and Horner Grocery, where he had stored his Popsicles. Free water was offered in paper cups, but the hardcore shoppers were intent on what was set next on the platform. Heads would snap when they brought out a new item. They had a chest of drawers there now with a mirror attached, and the auctioneer's wife read the description. Then the smooth voice of the auctioneer rumbled across the microphone. "Bidding starts with a thousand-dollar bill. Who wants to make it eleven hundred?"

No one batted an eye except me. Numbered cards flashed in the bright, summer afternoon, and hundred-dollar bills sprouted wings and flew out of deep pockets like soft, silky butterflies, light as air. Then the deep-throated voice of the auctioneer snatched them back into the action. "Now, who will make it twelve hundred?"

Edna and I watched. She watched the platform. I watched the people. Grace made a brief appearance one time with her clipboard as she directed some muscled, beefy boy to lift a table to the platform.

The crowd never wavered. Most of the movement was out of us—the locals. We tired easily, watching other people spend their money on furniture or whatnots that we had no use for at all. But we were fascinated, watching this strange human element, that much money being waved around so easily. None of them really knew what a dollar earned meant. The natives were pretty pleased with themselves. Maybe they felt they were in a good place right now. I know that's the way I felt then.

24

The Day After the Auction

There was still a crowd for breakfast on the day after the auction. A subdued table of men sat in the back and didn't have much to say. The visitors came by and filled the booths and most of the counter for early breakfast. Louise and I were hopping, and Mr. Rob even moved faster. Once the strangers gassed their big trucks and trailers, though, they hit the road. I was glad to see their taillights spinning out of sight. The money was good, but I was ready for a little dull routine.

After lunch, Edna stopped by and said they had a wild night at the Oasis. The place was packed, and some strangers got to ogling the Nuanz ladies a little too much. But nothing bad happened that she knew about as of now.

"I am getting too old for this, I reckon." Edna sat at the lunch counter after howdying the Liars' Table.

"Too old? For what? Living?" I didn't have time for a pity party today. Edna propped her chin with her hand and closed her eyes.

"Did you see a tall, thin dude in here yesterday before the sale? Kind of dirty-looking with weird eyes?"

"Yes. He fell asleep at the back corner table. Seemed like he was sick or scared, didn't know which."

"He was probably both."

"Did he come down to the bar last night?"

"He came in after midnight, and the place was full. He asked for a drink, not a beer, and said he wanted to stand on the front porch to drink it."

Edna shook her head. "I was standing there, and Moose looked at me. I nodded okay. Then I tried to explain to the guy, 'We can't really drink out in the open like that. But I know there's no place to sit right now.' He nodded his head like he understood."

She added, "I told him, 'Just stay back out of the light and then maybe there'll be something when you come back in.' The music was loud, and so was the talk. I couldn't quite make out what he said. But he paid for his drink and then turned with his cup and stood out against the building away from the streetlight. I didn't think anything about it. Until a little later, I noticed he was back standing three deep from the bar waiting for another drink. I was too busy to pay much more attention to him. The Hamilton boys were getting a little rowdy by then."

Edna waited for me to check out the last customer. Then she continued, "But Bonita came by a while ago wanting to know if I knew where he was. I said no. She was kind of worried about him. He kept trying to tell her something last night, and he talked so low she couldn't catch it all."

I asked her, "Why would that worry you?"

"She said he looked so sad." Edna shrugged her shoulders. "I told her I would keep my eye out for him today. But I haven't seen him anywhere. Have you?"

"No, we were busy this morning early, but I think I would have noticed if he came back in."

"Probably just a lonely old man going through some things."

"Well, there's plenty of those, aren't there?"

"Yeah. Who worries about the lonely ole women, I wonder?"

"I can tell you that. Nobody."

After that big sale, Mr. Salvatorre closed down the auction house for six weeks and took his lady friend with him. We settled back into our comfort zone and went about our own business. Joe was sailing again down the mighty Mississippi. I spent a lot of time gazing at the moon. Edna hung around a day or two, then hightailed it to Memphis.

The next day, they found Preacher's body on the Delacroix farm out west of town.

25

Preacher and Deacon—What a Pair

The next morning, the talk at the cafe was full of the murder. I caught bits of it until finally I stood at the men's table when Harry Collins came in. Harry and his friend Bill were the ones who found Preacher's body. They had been running their beagles on the back side of the Delacroix farm. Harry was probably my daddy's age. He was still big and robust from his college football days.

The other men at least waited for him to sit down before they started peppering him with questions.

Enjoying being the center of everyone's attention, Harry leaned back in his chair and pulled his coffee cup in front of him.

"Any idea who would have killed Preacher?" I asked.

"Sha. Could have been anybody. They beat on him pretty good first."

The men leaned in. "Sheriff got any leads?"

"None that he's telling. They're looking for Deacon now, though."

"He's that big guy, isn't he? Daddy used to work at the sale barn."

"Yeah. He and Preacher were a pair. Usually didn't see one without the other."

"Do they think he did it?"

"I dunno. When people are drugging, you don't know what they might do."

Harry cracked a smile then and sipped his coffee. "When we found Preacher, Bill took off faster than the dogs. I had to holler at him to help me get the dogs in the truck."

I listened as the guys started talking about Preacher and Deacon. I knew there would be some tales told. Mr. Graves seemed to know more about them than the others. They added bits and pieces to the discussion.

Preacher lived by the river next to the railroad trestle west of town for several months that last year of his life. A tall, thin man with pale skin and dark, greasy hair curling out from under a faded Cardinals baseball cap, Preacher talked incessantly.

"He could quote Scripture and poetry and snatches of songs. Sometimes it made sense; sometimes it didn't," Mr. Graves said. "He would sneak into town at night and steal what he could carry. Then he walked down the tracks with his supplies and slept underneath the trestle close to the river. That's where he did his drinking, drugging, and lighting fires at night. He used to say he was waiting for something." Everyone nodded.

Mr. Graves continued, "They called his sidekick Deacon. He is a big, burly guy with shoulder-length hair and a wide-scarred face. No one knows if it was from a knife fight or a fire, but he is pretty scary-looking—grim. Preacher used Deacon for the heavy-lifting jobs; they seemed to understand each other's purpose in their shared life."

"So how far out from town is the Delacroix place?"

"The railroad trestle is about half a mile from the courthouse as the crow flies."

No one said a word while I refilled coffee cups. I knew where they were talking about. I could hear the train whistle at night. I usually looked out west of town in the early evenings when I was on the roof. I knew that somebody was lighting fires sometimes down in the fields, but I had no idea if it was Preacher.

I couldn't sleep that night. All those stories about Preacher and Deacon kept hovering over me. The darkness was smothering. The downtown lights were blacked out after midnight. There was only starlight, and if the clouds drifted away, you could see the beginning of the fingernail moon midway between Orion's Sword and Betelgeuse. I walked down from my upstairs abode to sit on the cafe's front steps. After the excitement today, there was an ominous quietness over downtown. I heard a noise behind me then, like a garbage can rolling around, something heavy. There were no lights on at Mr. Harwood's office. Maybe a cat was prowling around.

I waited for a few seconds, calculating how many steps I would have to take back to the door. Then I heard a voice, a mumbling, sing-song pattern as if somebody was talking to themselves or warding off a bad spirit. I eased back to the doorway, but I waited to see if I heard it again. Maybe I had imagined it. I let out my breath, then heard it again. It seemed louder this time.

I opened the door to the staircase to my apartment, but I couldn't help myself. I eased behind the locked door and peeped through the window. The peeling sign stated, "No Solicitors," and the faded gilt letters of the Friedman Building left little space for me to see out. Just as I was ready to turn and go upstairs, a big head appeared. A man stood there with his back to me and peered at the courthouse clock. A car approached from the east side of the square, and the man stepped back into the shadow of the building and the doorway stoop. I ducked down and didn't move. The car lights faded, and suddenly I heard the man moan, a sound so full of pain and downright misery that it was almost animal-like. Then another moan was followed by some words with a rhythm like a phrase or a song.

"Whatcha gonna do? Let it go, let it go. Burning, burning. Whatcha gonna do?"

I sat with my back against the door, and his voice was so plaintive, so lonely, that I got enough nerve to peek out the window. All I could see was a big head full of hair. His back was to the door.

"Who is this?" I whispered. He kept swaying. Then my voice became stronger. "Who is this?" He jumped away from the door but didn't leave.

I hid my head but said louder, "Who are you? What do you want?"

He stayed there. I could hear him breathing. Finally he said, "This is Deacon. Who is you?"

"Never mind who I am. What are you doing?"

His voice cracked, and he started crying. "I don't know. I am looking for Preacher, but he's dead, I think. I don't know what to do."

On my tiptoes, I peeked at him. He stared at the door as if the door was talking to him.

"Deacon, this is Meshac from the cafe. What are you doing out here in the middle of the night?"

"I need some help, I reckon."

Of course, I unlocked the door.

Deacon stepped back from the stoop. I turned on the downstairs light. His clasped hands were in front of him as if he had been taught to stand like that when asking for something. His shoulders were hunched around his ears, and his long hair blew across his face. He didn't try to swipe it out of the way as he waited. I opened the door wide enough to be able to talk to him. My hip lodged against the door so I could close it quickly, I hoped.

"Hey," I said. "What do you want?"

He stood there a few seconds longer as if searching for the words he needed. His lips moved, but I couldn't hear anything.

"What did you say?"

"Can you help me?"

"Are you hurt? What's the matter?"

Deacon shook his head, and his hands went to his face. He began crying—big, racking, horrible cries that shook his body like a kid who has awakened from a nightmare. I didn't know what to do.

Finally, he caught his breath. He rubbed his face hard with his big, bony hands.

"I ain't et. I'm thirsty and tired. I guess I need to talk to somebody."

"You mean about Preacher?"

He nodded his head, and the tears rolled down his face again.

I couldn't help myself. "You wanna come in, Deacon?"

He nodded again but didn't move.

"Come on in and sit here on the staircase."

I held the door open for him. No cars were anywhere in sight.

He lumbered into the foyer. He had to be at least six feet four or six feet five, and I couldn't begin to guess how much he weighed. I could smell the fear on him, though, and he began to shiver like a hunting dog that senses he's nearly home or the hunt is over. His shoes were caked with mud, and his face was streaked with sweat. I led him over to the stairs against the wall and told him to sit down. His breathing was loud and rattling. I figured he had been balled up somewhere hiding all that time that Preacher lay out there, waiting for somebody to find him. I thought he could sure use a drink or something.

"You wanna tell me what happened, Deacon?"

He wrapped his arms around himself and shifted from one side to another. I thought he wasn't going to say anything, and then he spoke.

"Me and Preacher was buddies. He could do the talking, and I could do the walking. That's what we said. Talking and walking, you know. Me and him, we was buddies."

He drew a long sigh in and out, and his big body trembled. I thought he might start crying again.

"Want some coffee?"

He stared at me and nodded his head.

"Stay down here, and I'll bring you some."

I went upstairs to the kitchen, started a pot of coffee, and searched in the cabinets for some cookies or crackers or anything. I didn't hear a sound the whole time I was in the kitchen. When I made my way back with the coffee tray and some old Oreo cookies, I half expected him to be gone or asleep. But he was just staring at the floor with his arms wrapped around himself. He took the hot coffee and gulped two big swallows. It didn't seem to faze him. He started talking then, and I sat down beside him and listened.

"Me and Preacher, we had us a hideout underneath the railroad trestle. If we couldn't find a place to sleep in town, we'd head out there and make us a fire and get under our cardboard and plywood if it was cold. Some nights we'd get separated, and I wouldn't find him until it got light. Preacher always knew where we could sleep at night, and if I lost him, then I was just on my own. He told me that, and he was right."

His big hand held the stack of Oreos, and he paused long enough to shove three or four into his mouth.

"So a while back, we had been hanging out in the vacant building next to the Oasis because there weren't nobody living in the house anymore. It had thick walls, and we'd found some piles of old tarps and blankets and could get in easy enough. We didn't think nobody had seen us there, but we was wrong. That night, somebody came and started beating on the door and hollering. We run out the back, but somebody was standing there, too, with a light shining in our eyes.

"Somebody hit me on the back of my head. I remember falling on the floor. Somebody kicked me in the ribs. When I woke up, Preacher was gone. Hit was still dark. I walked over to Pee Wee's house, and he let me come in till it got light."

He stopped and shook his head.

"I had blood all over me, and I was scared something had happened to Preacher, since he was gone and all."

He finished off the cookies and emptied the last of the coffee.

"Once it got light, I started walking down the track, but I couldn't find Preacher nowhere. There was some canned viennas and beans hid under the trestle. I ate them out of the can, I was so hungry. I guess I slept awhile, and when I woke up, it was getting dark and raining again. I didn't know what to do without Preacher, so I was just sitting there when I heard something over in the persimmon grove back behind me. I got down low on the ground and tried to hide when I heard some men talking. They had baseball bats and they was walking along the ditch, hitting the bushes with those bats and cussing and all. I couldn't make out who they was, but I crawled away and then ran as fast as I could toward the road. I caught a ride into town and spent the night kind of walking around—like I do, you know."

I had no idea when this happened, and I was afraid if I stopped him to try and figure it out, he would lose his thought.

"Go on, what happened next?"

"Well, I was hanging outside Miss Edna's place. You know the Oasis up there?"

I nodded.

"Sometimes she would set out some leftovers for us underneath the backdoor stoop if she had something. My stomach was growling, and I didn't know how I was gonna eat. She had set out a carton of stew and wrapped some cornbread in a napkin. I was leaning against the wall, eating like a hog, when she came out. Miss Edna. And she asked me where Preacher was. I just shook my head. I was scared to tell her 'bout them chasing us and all."

I didn't know what to say, so I waited.

"She told me some men had been looking for Preacher, and they was pretty mad at him. I told her I hadn't seen him for two nights. Miss Edna told me I better watch where I went 'cause she was afraid something might happen to me and Preacher. That's when I decided to go back out there."

Deacon had eaten the Oreos by then, so I made a quick trip upstairs to get him a sleeve of crackers and some cheese. He ate like a robot, just automatically reaching out and pushing it into his mouth. I don't think he tasted a thing.

"Did you see them hurt Preacher?"

He startled when I said Preacher's name. He took a deep breath.

"No'm, but I saw him dead." His mouth started trembling again. "I was walking everywhere looking for him like Miss Edna said, down there by the tracks underneath the trestle and then up and down the fields and in the ditches. Somebody had scattered all our stuff all over and tried to burn it. I kept walking and looking. Then I saw a pile of something, but I didn't know for sure if it was him or not."

He stopped talking then, and his face turned even whiter.

"I saw Preacher's cap there and I called out to him, 'Preacher, is that you?' But he didn't move. Not a tall. I knew it wasn't no use to go over there. He was good and dead. I started walking back to the river.

I crossed it, and I stayed there even when I heard the sirens and all the commotion. I stayed there behind that big sycamore waiting for them to come after me. Nobody ever did."

We sat for a few minutes. The light from the square created the window-frame pattern on the floor. Deacon was like a part of the stairs, solid and immovable, like a mountain with a crack down its side.

"So, when it started getting dark, I walked by the railroad tracks toward town. I got close enough I could see the clock on the courthouse lit like the moon. I crossed the tracks and got me a good drink of water at the fountain there. Preacher used to say it was the coldest water in town—right next to the water plant and all. Then I walked straight through the back lots following the clock's light. Didn't nobody see me, I'm pretty sure—till I ran over the trash cans there in the alley."

He sat there as if he was all talked out. I stretched out my hand and asked if he wanted more coffee.

"No'm. I guess I need to go talk to the sheriff?" The words ended in a question to me.

"Probably so. Want me to go with you?"

"That'd be good."

The sheriff's office was a couple of blocks off the court square. I locked the door, and we took our time getting there. The closer we came, the more upset Deacon grew. He stopped at the corner by the car dealer's building. He started rocking back and forth, his hands deep in his worn parka. His foot tapped on the sidewalk. He muttered something like "burning night." I couldn't place it, but it was familiar. Then he stopped and said, "Follow me."

He took off toward the depot and I followed, cutting across the parking lots, with the dark buildings looming above us.

We started down the alley, then got close to Edna's Oasis, which was dark. Even the neon palm trees in the windows were dimmed. Then he disappeared right before my eyes.

"Deacon." I was careful not to be too loud. "Deacon, where are you?"

I listened for any sound of movement or breathing. Then I heard footsteps and felt a whoosh of air. My heart beat ratchety-rack against my ribcage. Suddenly, Deacon was there again.

"Come on," he said. He reached toward me, but I stepped away.

"Go on. I lost you for a minute."

That's when he led me to a little side door in the old lumberyard building. The back of an abandoned house was not six feet away. The windows shone in the dark, but there was no other movement anywhere. The metal door scraped against the broken concrete as Deacon pulled it with all his might. He walked in and then turned to me.

"Come on, I got something to show you."

It was so dark inside I couldn't see my hand in front of me.

"Deacon," I whispered. "I can't see a dang thing."

He reached and tugged on my shirt sleeve, pulling me along but not touching me at all. My eyes adjusted some, but I still couldn't tell what, if anything, was inside. Suddenly, Deacon let go of me, and I froze.

"Wait here."

I could hear him opening a door or a cabinet, scuffling along with some rustling of boxes or papers maybe. Then he shined a small pen light toward me. It blinded me, but at least there was some light now. I walked toward him.

"This here's where me and Preacher been sleeping some nights. Preacher said it was pretty safe here in town next to Miss Edna's place. The front door is locked, but we managed to squeeze in this door."

Deacon let the light bounce around the room, over the concrete floor, up the walls, and across the ceiling. Then he pointed the light on a pile of boxes and blankets, bolts of cloth, and brown paper. A broken chair with no legs, just a seat, leaned against the wall. He walked over and, holding the light in his mouth, rummaged through the wooden box underneath the stacks. I stood close but not too close.

Deacon kept mumbling. He reached inside a bent metal box and pulled out a dirty old Crown Royal sack with the strings drawn tight across the top. He swung it around in front of me and took the light out of his mouth.

"Would you keep this for me?"

I stuck out my hand. "I will keep the sack for you. Come by when you want it."

Whatever was in the sack was heavy and twisted around with the weight. The dirty gold string was tied in several knots, and I had no idea what on earth I was keeping for him.

Deacon nodded his head. "Good."

He turned off the light, caught hold of my sleeve again, and started back toward the door. I was glad to hear the metal door creak and scrape across the concrete floor. We walked back onto the quiet street. But I felt better than in the blackness behind us. As I started toward the square, Deacon disappeared. I don't know how somebody that big could move that fast. Maybe my heart was thumping so loudly that I didn't hear his footsteps, but it was almost like he evaporated into the night, soundless like a giant night bird.

I didn't even call out his name. I unlocked and locked the door and made my way to my apartment. I put the oddly shaped bag at the back of my closet and tried to forget it was even there.

My apartment was hot and stuffy. I walked across the lobby and climbed the fire escape. The moon had risen nearly directly over me. The night was quiet and still, and I knew in my bones that something wasn't right in Nuanz. I wondered what was beginning here.

The days after Preacher was murdered and Deacon didn't reappear fell one upon each other like stacks of wood. I didn't ask too many questions, like why. I don't know what the others were thinking. Routines are good for getting through hard times. Sometimes that's all we have.

26

The Return of Edna

The rest of that week dragged by. Suddenly, Edna Love was there, coming in the front door of the Bluebird Cafe. I did a double take when she walked over to the lunch counter. She resembled Miss Kitty after the rustlers captured and held her in that cabin in the woods.

"Edna?" I couldn't say another word. She fell on the first stool she could find.

"Edna, are you all right?"

She shook her head. I poured her some coffee and pushed the cup and saucer to her. All the fire was dead in her eyes. My God, she had gray streaks in her hair.

"What's the matter, Edna?"

She didn't say a word, and when she reached for her coffee, her hand shook. I swear it did. I got closer to her face. I thought maybe she was drunk.

"What are you doing, Mesha?"

"Nothing, Edna, just glad to see you. Where have you been?"

I waited for her to whisper some dark and daring story.

"What do you mean?" she said, hanging her head and splaying her hands on the counter.

"I haven't seen you in a week. Everybody's been looking for you."

She raised her eyes. They looked blank, turned inward toward something only she saw.

"Edna, you want to go to my apartment and lay down?"

She didn't say a word but stood and gripped her purse. I hollered at Mr. Rob, "I'm taking a break." I grabbed a hold of her arm. She stumbled a minute, then righted herself. The men at the back table stared. No one said a word.

"Come on, let's go upstairs."

I helped her out the door. She linked her arm inside mine as I opened the Friedman Building door, and we trudged upstairs, one footworn step after another. Little Tom peered out the office window at me, but I shook my head once.

Edna didn't say a word and waited while I unlocked the door. She paused inside my apartment as if she was in a strange land.

"Do you need to lie down?'

She nodded her head, dropped her purse, and headed toward my bed. She flopped on top of the coverlet with her head buried in the pillows. Her muddy shoes hung off the side of the bed, and her body was catty-cornered across the bedspread.

"I am taking your shoes off."

She remained silent. I slipped off the shoes. She curled on her side, then closed her eyes and fell asleep.

"I don't know what's happened, Edna, but you're safe here. I promise."

Edna was in a dead sleep. I didn't know what to do next, but I knew Mr. Rob would be hollering soon if I didn't get back. I took her purse and threw it into my closet, lowered the blinds, and left the light on in the bathroom. Surely, she would know where she was when she woke up. I trucked back to the cafe and made it through the supper hour.

It was still light out when I told Lottie to close for me, and I traipsed back upstairs. I had no idea if Edna would still be there, but when I got inside, I wasn't too shocked to see she was still asleep. I set some leftovers on the kitchen counter and tiptoed around the best I could. I could have screamed, "Fire," and Edna wouldn't have stirred.

I ate some fried potatoes and squash before they got too cold, along with a hunk of cornbread. There was just enough milk in the fridge for one glass, and I drank that down. I sat there, then rocked and wondered what on earth Edna Love had been into. She cried out once. Her legs jumped a bit, and then she was quiet. I didn't want to disturb her, so I dragged the extra blanket out of the closet and slipped the rocker cushion underneath my head. I didn't think I would sleep, but the thousand steps, the poured cups, and the hello, goodbye, and thank-you all rose and laid me flat.

When I woke up a little after midnight, the moonlight played across Edna's body in my bed, and a sequined chopstick flickered. She had not moved as far as I could tell. I dared not touch her, but I stood beside the bed and watched to be sure she was alive. She was. I knew my back would be sore from sleeping on the floor all night, but I couldn't figure out how to squeeze in next to her without waking her.

I believe I can do without some shut-eye for one night, I thought.

The curtain sighed and billowed out like the pursed lips of a sleeping baby. I lay there wide awake for hours, wondering what, if any, plan I needed to make. Then suddenly, the bedsprings squeaked. I opened my eyes, and Edna was sitting in the middle of my bed. Her face was gray and creased across her left cheek. Her hair swayed in the air like a dangerous mountain peak.

I whispered, "Edna . . . Edna, it's me, Mesha."

I thought for a minute she didn't recognize me. She sat there staring into space, then covered her face with her hands. I stood beside the bed and waited.

She mumbled into her hands, "What day is it?"

"It's Thursday morning. The sun's not up yet."

She sat there for a minute. "No, what day of the month is it?"

I had to look at the calendar. "It's the sixteenth? Fifteenth? Of July."

"Are you sure?"

I looked again. "Yes, it's July 15. Where have you been, Edna?"

She sat there, rubbing her fingers into her temples like she had a headache. I didn't know what to do.

"Can I stay here today?"

"Sure you can. Stay as long as you like." I waited a minute, then asked, "Do you want something to eat?"

Edna stared right through me as if I weren't there. Then she shook her head, her eyes studying my apartment, and slowly lay back down straight in the bed, her head on my pillow.

"Come on over here if you want to sleep. That floor must be . . ."

She never finished the sentence. I crept closer and peered at her. She was on her side, her back to me and the door. I sat down slowly on the bed. I had a couple more hours before work. Not thinking I would sleep, I was shocked when the alarm rang. I jumped to turn it off. For a moment, I forgot about my bed partner, and when I saw that lump, I nearly screamed. She had drawn the bedspread on her side and was dead to the world.

I moved around as quietly as I could. I put on my work clothes, brushed my teeth and hair, and quietly closed and locked the door. Edna could throw the bolt when she got up if she wanted to go home.

I sat on the stairs and put on my shoes before I stepped into my daytime world. I tried to leave Edna and her dilemma away from me and prying eyes and ears. That wouldn't be easy.

I tried to keep an eye outside the cafe window to see if I caught a glimpse of her leaving, but we were busy all the way through breakfast and lunch. She certainly hadn't made an appearance on purpose. I half expected the sheriff to appear and start quizzing me, but he didn't. The men who saw Edna yesterday in that state never said a word to me, but I felt them watching me as we waited for the door to usher in Edna Love.

Lolly came in for the early dinner crowd, and I told her and Mr. Rob that I would see them tomorrow. I packed an extra helping of vegetable soup, a couple of rolls, and one leftover chicken thigh in a paper sack. When I got to my apartment door, I was nervous. I didn't know if I wanted Edna to be there or not. I got out my keys but twisted the doorknob first. It held fast. She must still be there. I adjusted my face and attitude, and when no one responded to my noise, I unlocked the door and opened it wide.

Though dark inside, the dim light from the window showed my tiny home. The bed covers were wadded with sheets hanging over the side touching the floor. There was the smell of cigarettes and grease mingled with a drop of something—fear, I think. Edna sat in my rocker, moving only her feet back and forth, so the rocker nodded and creaked slightly. She didn't turn her head when I came in.

"Good evening, Edna."

She continued to rock. I stood there. At last, she stared at me with blank eyes, and I was crushed. My heart raced, and the pulse in my neck jumped like crazy. She didn't say a word. Her gaze drifted past me over my shoulder. "Did you lock the door?"

I turned and checked the lock.

"Yes, it's locked."

She began rocking again. The darkness drifted in. I moved to the kitchen counter, turned on a feeble light, and began straightening the apartment. I ran the sink full of water, threw the few dishes into the suds, swiped the counter with the dishrag, and walked to the bed. I straightened the covers and fluffed the pillows but left it unmade.

Then I sat on the edge of the bed and gave Edna the once-over. My hero. My tower of strength. The original queen-pin if there ever was one. Frankly, she looked old, puffy, and given out. I waited as long as I could. Then, leaning back on my arms casually, I said, "What do you want me to do?"

She mumbled, "I could use a good cup of coffee."

I grinned, but she didn't. I made a pot and waited to hear the perking and smell the scent of fresh coffee.

"Do you want something to eat?"

"No, just coffee."

I carried her cup over and set it on the table beside the rocker. She reached for the cup and held it close to her bosom. The steam wandered toward her face. She stretched out her legs and lay back against the rocker. I thought she wasn't ready to talk yet. When she spoke, her voice was husky. I strained to hear her.

"Some say the third day is a good day for a resurrection."

She bit her lower lip. Her shoulders inched up close to her ears.

"All I wanted was to be in love …"

She sounded wistful, a longing deep inside. ". . . One more time before I die."

I didn't know what to say. She brought the cup to her lips, blew across the top, and took a tentative sip. I don't know if she even tasted a drop. She was going through the motions as if something ordinary could bring her out of this blur.

"I met this man a couple of months ago when I went to Memphis. Remember? I think it was February, and I was going stir crazy?"

I nodded my head.

"I got a room at the Peabody. The manager is a friend of mine. I went down for a drink in the bar. This guy kept giving me the eye, which wasn't so unusual. But I wasn't in the mood, you know."

She took another sip of coffee.

"I called for my bill, and the waitress said it was paid and nodded to the guy sitting there by himself. I nodded back, but I didn't wander over to thank him personally." Edna started the rocker again and then stopped.

"The next day, he was there in the dining room. I thought I better thank him personally, so I did. Nothing pinged when I studied him. There was nothing at all about him that stirred anything in me. I felt no attraction, no thoughts of pursuing this a bit more. I geared up for a day of shopping and pounded that pavement in the big city. But that was how it started."

She stared into her cup, and I waited for her. She sipped on her coffee.

"That doesn't sound too bad. Is that where you disappeared to all this spring to see him?"

Edna shifted in her seat and drained the coffee. "If you only knew. I was taken on a royal ride, and there's no one to blame but me."

"What do you mean?"

"He has done a number on me. Big time. I fell hook, line, and sinker for it all."

She started crying again. Big, deep, heavy sobs. Her face turned red, and the tears poured down her face and dropped in her lap. She bent over and held her head in her hands. I didn't know what to do but let her cry. Eventually, I leaned over and patted her like she was Grace or somebody's kid.

"Edna, it's gonna be all right. We'll figure this out, I promise."

Good Lord, I thought. *What on earth am I going to do now?*

Edna seemed better after her come-apart. I warmed the soup and the chicken thigh and toasted some cheese and crackers. We sat together at the table with the windows open. I could hear the courthouse clock and counted the strikes as always. This time was nine times. Oh ye of little faith. It was nine o'clock in downtown Nuanz. A word from God maybe? Was that an answer?

"Can I stay one more night?" Edna's voice was so low that I had to ask her to repeat herself.

"Of course. You can stay the rest of your life if you want."

She smiled then. "Let's don't get carried away."

But she was out of her dazed state, so that was good. I figured I would learn the rest of the story when she was ready, but I just wanted her to get back to being Edna Love.

It's funny how when you're alone for so long, you think you would give anything to have somebody in your life to love and love you back. The silence of living alone gets under my skin sometimes. But when you're used to being alone with your thoughts, and another person is there, you can't think straight. It's all about them. Having Edna there in my apartment was strange. I thought Edna had everything and everybody figured out. This may have been a hard lesson for both of us to learn.

I left Edna in my bed the next morning, and by eight o'clock, she opened the cafe door and stood there. She was dressed in a new set of clothes with her hair pooched high.

"Hon, I'm on my way to Connie's to get my roots touched up." She cocked her head to one side and shrugged her shoulders. As she walked toward the square, those shiny black chopsticks in her hair reached toward the courthouse all by themselves. I swear I saw a blue crackle of light that jumped skyward toward the clock tower like a damn electric arc. *Thank God*, I thought. Maybe everything would be all right.

PART IV
TIGERS AND MOONFLOWERS

Henry's Vigil

Henry Malone sat on the sidewalk outside the courthouse and stared at the clock tower. For several days, people walked around him. Sometimes he moved over into the shade, but he never took his eyes off the clock.

He disappeared at night but reappeared as soon as the sun rose. I watched him from time to time because things didn't feel right in downtown Nuanz. Something hovered over us. That's not all that unusual, I have discovered.

Henry belonged to Lawyer Malone, whose office was across the street from the Bluebird Cafe. Maybe he had come to town with Mr. Malone and was hanging out—waiting for him to emerge from the courthouse.

But knowing Henry, we thought something was peculiar when he kept staring at the clock tower. On his way to the courthouse, Lawyer Malone would stop and chat with Henry, but the dog mainly lay or sat there in the same spot on the south side, looking up.

After that week passed, he came for a few hours every day and then went on to other adventures. We speculated—did Henry have something cornered? Was he waiting for us to figure it out? Did Henry know something we didn't know? Probably.

When a dog can sense what he needs like Henry can, why can't we humans figure that out? Instinct has saved many. Some call it a gut feeling. A shiver of fear or an ominous forewarning—that comes from within us humans. No matter how educated or uneducated we are—that push to act, run, or hide—it's there if we're paying attention.

The events of the past few weeks had us paying attention, I hoped. I knew I was. I was sure Henry was, too.

28

Johnny and the Oasis

For the next couple of weeks, Edna continued not to be herself. She went through the motions, but I could tell something gnawed at her. She wasn't standoffish, but she played a part that she thought I needed to see.

Tonight, I was stopping by the Oasis to see if I could get her to talk to me. After work, I changed out of my waitress clothes and walked the couple of blocks. The lights were on like old times. Inside, the usual crowd was there. Moose was behind the bar. Johnny, Jesse, and Robert were on the far side nursing their beers. The jukebox was playing, not too loud, and smoke lay over the crowd like a blanket.

Moose grinned. "Hey, little lady, haven't seen you in a while."

"I know. I been kind of busy. Is Edna here?"

"She'll be back in a few."

I slid in next to Johnny.

"The usual?"

I laughed. "Yeah, give me a good cup of coffee. Emphasis on good."

Moose poured out the remains of the coffeepot and then started a new pot for me.

"So, Johnny, what have you been up to?"

"Oh, nothing much, Mesha, rescuing damsels in distress mainly."

Johnny chuckled and sipped his beer. I noticed he had a bandage on his hand.

"What happened to your hand?"

"No big deal. I banged it on something."

There was a slight pink tinge to his thumb underneath all the gauze, and three of his fingers were wrapped in one solid swoop.

"Looks pretty bad."

He laid his hand in his lap and shifted in his seat. He leaned back and tried to look at ease. Johnny has always been quiet and kind of nervous like a cat. He could fade into the background, and you would forget he was there. But I had learned that he knew a whole lot about what was going on in town. You had to pull it out of him, but he could feel the rumblings underneath us. People didn't put enough stock in what he said, but I did. He began drumming his right fingers on the counter, unaware he was even doing that.

I leaned over to speak to Jesse and Robert. They spoke but barely. I guessed they hadn't had enough to drink yet. Slow day.

After a while, I felt Johnny looking at me.

"What?" I asked.

Johnny and I had crossed paths several times since I moved to Nuanz. I knew how loyal he was to Edna, and I knew that he would protect her if he could.

He leaned over and propped his bandaged hand on the side of his face to keep Jesse from hearing him.

"Have you seen Edna today?"

"No, I haven't. That's one reason I am here now."

He nodded and looked straight ahead.

"What's going on with her?" I asked. "She hasn't been the same since she came back from that last jaunt."

"I can't figure it out. She don't talk to me like she used to."

"You know she was in bad shape when she showed up. Slept about twelve hours solid in my bed."

"Yeah, I heard."

". . . But she never explained it all to me."

Johnny shook his head.

"There's something not right." He took a long sip of his beer.

"Have you asked her?"

"No, I wouldn't ask her outright. None of my business, but I saw her Cadillac down on Paradise Alley early one morning." He held up his beer to let Moose know he was ready for another. He leaned on his elbows.

"Edna doesn't do early mornings unless it's the end of a late night."

"Do you think she's bit off more than she can chew?"

We both shook our heads.

"I don't think that's possible, is it?"

Johnny paused a minute. "Nah, no way."

"Guess we'll have to wait and see."

My coffee was about gone by then. I thought I might have to go before I saw Edna, but lo and behold, then she walked in the door.

She smiled a big greeting. "Hello."

Everyone lifted their hands or drinks to her. She sauntered over and set her purse on the counter. "What's going on, girlie?"

"Oh, nothing, I been missing Johnny here, so I thought I might find him at the Oasis."

She laughed and nodded her head to Moose to pour her one.

"Well, you found him."

We laughed, and the lights seemed to brighten a bit.

"Looks like Johnny here has been into something he shouldn't have." I took my coffee refill from Moose.

Edna cut her eyes at Johnny. He stuck his hand down below the counter again.

"What do you mean?"

"Well, looks like he nearly lost a finger or two."

"Hush, Mesha," he said.

Edna asked, "What happened?"

Johnny said, "None of your business, ma'am."

I laughed and then realized I was the only one laughing. Edna walked back to her office. Not a word. Johnny put a couple of dollars down and stood to leave.

"Wow, Johnny, what'd I do?"

"Oh, nothing. I gotta go."

He left before I could say another word. After I finished my coffee and paid, I walked back to Edna's office. The door was closed, but I pushed against it. Edna was slumped forward, her folded arms on her desk. Her head was down like a kid at school who has been punished. The door creaked as I pushed it open, but she didn't move. I stood in the doorway a minute, and when she didn't respond, I closed the door behind me.

When I walked to the end of the block, Johnny was sitting on the steps leading to Mr. Cunningham's store, which was locked for the night. Obviously, he was waiting for me. I lowered myself to the top step beside him.

"What's going on, Johnny?"

He wouldn't look straight at me. He shrugged his shoulders and tapped the ashes off his cigarette.

"I better tell you about my hand."

"Okay." I waited.

"About a week ago, when Edna was gone for a few days, I kept seeing a car with an out-of-state license plate in town. Different places but usually after dark. I didn't think anything at first, but then I wondered why." He took another drag on his cigarette.

"I made sure I walked by the Oasis a few times when I was out and about. On the third night, I was ready to forget it when I smelled something. There was smoke coming up from the walk-through there by the club."

He turned then and pointed over his shoulder. "See there on the far corner past the back door?"

I turned and saw where he was pointing. Yeah.

"There's just enough room between them two buildings for a man to walk down. Right in the middle was a stack of wood and some boxes on fire. I didn't think I had time to call for help, so I took off my jacket and tried smothering the fire, beating with my hands and stomping. I finally got that dang fire out, but I burned my fingers on my left hand pretty good."

"Geez, Johnny, I'm sorry. But why didn't you tell somebody?"

"Who was there to tell?"

"I don't know, but maybe Edna needs to know."

He shook his head. "Nope, I'm watching and trying to figure out who did it and why. But I need you to stay quiet about my hand." He smiled then.

"Of course. Me and my big mouth. I'm sorry. But keep me posted. I see and hear a lot of things at the cafe, you know."

"Oh, I will."

Johnny flipped his cigarette down past the curb. He headed toward Depot Street.

As I walked toward the square, the clock tower was shining at me like another closer moon. There was a chill in the air that shouldn't have been there on a late July evening. I didn't know what to do next, but I better do something. Edna was too important to all of us. Plus, that last time, she appeared in such a bedraggled shape that threw me and half the town for a loop.

Edna was always on top of everything. If she was losing herself, what on earth was going to happen to the rest of us? I kept waiting for the real Edna to show, but she was struggling with something. At first, she didn't even try to pretend things were all right. Now she was just keeping to herself.

The next time I saw Edna, she seemed more like her old self. Those earrings were dangling, and there was not a sign of gray anywhere in her stacked-high French twist hairdo. I waited for her to tell me what else happened in Memphis, but she was all business whenever I was around her. I had other things on my mind, too.

29

Deacon's Demise

One morning, the sheriff came and sat at the Liars' Table in the back. Mr. Gordon started the conversation. "How's the investigation coming along about Preacher?"

The others turned and looked at the sheriff.

"Not much going on right now. We can't find Deacon, for one thing. Preacher's family wrote him off a long time ago. They were no help at all."

I set the expected cup of coffee in front of the sheriff. He nodded his head.

"Any of you seen Preacher and Deacon in the last couple of months?"

Mr. Hockaday said, "They were hanging out at Depot Street somewhere. I would meet them near there lots of times as I left town."

Mr. Gordon added, "Edna used to give them odd jobs every once in a while and some food when things got thin."

Several nodded their heads. The sheriff rubbed the back of his neck. "I talked to Edna but didn't get much help there. There's a couple of empty buildings in the next block from the Oasis."

I couldn't help myself—I lingered by the table eavesdropping.

"My deputy said somebody had pried open the back door. But we didn't find anything there."

"Which building is that?" someone asked.

"The one facing the alley. The grass was mashed down, and some old blood was on the floor."

"Who's storing stuff in the printing building there?"

Lawyer Malone spoke up. "That's part of the Salvatorre auctions now. He stores different pieces there between auctions."

The door opened, and Mr. Graves hurried inside to see what he was missing.

One of the men said, "Harry and Bill were pretty shook finding Preacher and all."

"It was a pretty brutal scene. Somebody was looking for something— something of value." The sheriff tapped his cup with one finger for a refill.

Mr. Know-It-All McHugh piped up. "Whoever it was must not have known Preacher. I never knew him to have anything that was worth anything at all."

No one said another word about the murder. Conversation soon turned to the weather and the usual coffee talk. I kept my ears open and my mouth closed.

As dawn cracked the following Sunday, Edna called. "I need you to meet me at the Nuanz Motor Inn in about thirty minutes."

She sounded like she was in a hurry. I told her I'd be there. Luckily, this was my Sunday off.

She parked her Caddy about the same time I got there. Dawn was chilly, but Edna had a sheen on her upper lip, and she sounded a little wheezy.

"What's going on?"

"Deacon. I need to move him somewhere safer."

"You've got Deacon?"

"He knocked on my back door a few days ago, and I moved him to the country for a while. But he's not safe anymore."

"What's the matter?"

"He's been beat up pretty bad. I think it had something to do with Guido."

"Mr. S? What are you talking about?"

At that, Deacon peeked his big, shaggy head up from the back seat and gave me a fright. His face was covered in bruises, and his eyes were swollen shut. He tried to smile, but his busted lip cracked open, and blood trickled down the side of his mouth.

"Hell, lay back down, Deacon."

I looked around to see if anybody saw us.

"Hidey, Miz."

"Deacon, who did this to you?"

"I don't know. But they're looking for it."

"For what?"

"I can't remember what I done with it."

He lay back down and fell asleep. Edna leaned against the car.

"Got any ideas where we could hide him? I don't need him to be too near me."

"Is the sheriff still looking for him?"

Edna didn't answer.

"What are we going to do with him?"

"I need to keep him hidden for a few more days till I figure this out."

"Give me a couple of hours. I might can arrange something with Queen."

I walked to Rem's, which was locked, and tiptoed over to the back part of Queen's house. I couldn't hear anything inside, so I knocked quietly. Nothing. I waited a few beats and knocked again. Then I tried as quietly as I could to call Queen's name.

"Queen, it's me. Meshac."

I walked around the corner to see if any lights were on. I didn't want to go on the porch.

I pecked on the window. "Queen, it's Meshac." Suddenly, the window shade flew up.

"What in the hell are you doing down here at dark thirty on a Sunday morning?"

Queen didn't look too queenly to me. Her hair stood straight off her head, and her eyes were all squinched.

"Let me in. I need some help."

She pulled the shade down, and I huddled against the back of the house. I heard footsteps across the porch, and she opened the screen door.

"Get in here. This better be good."

She scratched her head, peering at me. "What have you got going on now, girl?"

"It's Edna and Deacon."

"Oh, my lord. That druggie that killed Preacher?"

"We don't know that he killed Preacher."

"That's what the talk is. And what's Edna got to do with this?"

"You know Edna; she's in everything."

Queen rolled her eyes. "Come in here and let me get some coffee."

I followed her into the kitchen as she started a pot of coffee. She shook her head. "Girl, you have got to stop snooping around in everybody's business. Haven't you learned your lesson?"

"I know. But how do you tell Edna no?"

I explained the Deacon situation and asked if there was a place where we could put him for a few days.

"I don't know what Edna's doing, but she'll work everything out."

Queen sipped her coffee and stared out the window. "Let me talk to Noc and see what we can do."

"Thanks. I owe you."

"Big time."

By seven o'clock, I had met up with Edna again. Noc told Queen to take Deacon to Paradise Alley across from Madam's house. They picked me up behind the Friedman Building. I directed Edna the long way around so nobody would see us.

"We need to come in the back way through that lane off Christmasville Road. Head back out to the motel. Queen gave me the directions."

Edna took off, and Deacon lay in the back seat. We passed the motel in a little ways.

"Here, take this dirt road to the right there. Turn here."

The Caddy bounced over a couple of huge washouts. In one place, there was a ditch across half the road. Edna swung the car over and hit the edge of the hole. My head flew up and hit the car roof. We wound around several more back roads. The gravel dust funneled behind us like a cyclone. Cows turned their heads as we zipped past.

The last house on the far edge of Paradise Alley had been empty all spring with a "no trespassing" sign nailed to the front door. There was a shed on the back of the lot, and Noc said that nobody should bother Deacon there. The river lay a hundred yards or so north. Thick, overgrown woods were behind the shed. Inside the shed was a broken chair with an old fold-up cot in the corner and a trunk full of blankets. We settled Deacon in the little room near the back door. I brought him some food and water to clean up a bit. The current was off.

Deacon was even more disoriented. He cried and moaned, then drifted off. His sleeping was fitful, and he would roar sometimes like he was scared to death. He sat straight once and said, "It's the wampus. Make it go away, Preacher."

Edna tried talking to him, but he didn't seem to know who she was. We sat there with him until he settled down. Edna told him he needed to lay low and not let anybody in but us. Then we left him there.

Edna drove us to my apartment, and we climbed the stairs. She paced back and forth in my kitchen.

"I'm kind of on the hook about finding this item for Mr. S."

"What do you think Deacon has to do with it?"

"All I know is Guido told me before he left town that Deacon's name had come up about some items missing from the gallery."

I nearly broke out in a cold sweat then. Deacon's words haunted me. *Would you keep something for me?*

I knew then that I needed to drag out the Crown Royal bag. I went to the closet and pulled out the tin box with the bag lying there on top.

"Shit. What's that?" Edna asked.

I told her how Deacon had given it to me the night after Preacher was murdered. I had not opened it. She glared at me with those bamboo chopsticks pointing straight up.

"When were you going to tell me about this?"

"I don't know. I was kind of waiting to see if Deacon showed up."

She glared at me with one hand on her hip. "Well, open it."

I pulled the bag from the box and carried it to the kitchen table. The faded gold strings were pulled tight, double-tied in old, dry knots. I struggled with it.

"Just cut the dang thing," she said.

I grabbed my kitchen knife and sawed the strings apart. My fingers trembled, and I grabbed the cinched opening and pulled it apart. A musty smell floated out as I opened the purple sack.

I felt metal, and as my fingers wrapped around the shape, my heart was pounding.

I pulled out a heavy bronze sculpture that landed with a thud on the table. The sculpture was a tiger prowling with its tail in midswing and its head low. I held my breath. The Bugatti. The one that Mr. S had been waiting on. It had been in my closet all this time.

"Is this what Mr. S is looking for?"

All I could do was nod my head.

"Look on the bottom and see if it's signed."

"Yep. R. Bugatti. Rembrandt Bugatti. Remember what I told you about him?"

Edna nodded her head; then we both stared at the tiger.

"Is this the real thing?"

"I would say so. And worth a damn fortune."

I tried to take a deep breath. My voice squeaked. "The Bugatti was here in my piddly-ass closet all this time. Oh my God. What do you think it's worth?"

"Guido wouldn't say exactly, but he had this look in his eye when he told me he needed it found quick."

We couldn't take our eyes off the statue.

"Some of this guy's stuff runs over two hundred grand."

"Yeah, I know. He committed suicide. Of course, that always makes stuff more valuable when an artist dies a tragic death."

I stood with my arms folded, looking at that lump of metal that had been molded into a fiery tiger years ago, way over there across the ocean in Italy, by Rembrandt Bugatti's hands. His eyes saw the tiger pacing in its cage or roaming in the jungle. His hands followed each muscle, the head, the ears, the deep-set eyes, the skin stretched over the shoulders, its rump, its paws. Here on my rickety kitchen table in Nuanz, Tennessee, sat a tiger created by Bugatti. He formed this tiger with his artist hands and suffering heart. Bugatti's intention was there in the tiger. I could see it. I could feel it.

Somehow, this tiger crossed the ocean and landed here. The light glinted off the bronze. Edna was struck dumb—a state foreign to her. I ran my fingers over the back and felt the shape of this powerful cat. I touched where Bugatti's hands had molded this tiger's nature with his human understanding. He spoke for the tiger. His understanding with the tiger's raw nature was evident. I could almost feel the rumble of the tiger's growl.

"Tyger, Tyger burning bright." I could hear my teacher's voice reading to a roomful of bored seventh-graders and Mr. S's voice whispering those same lines.

"What do we do now?"

"Well, the sculpture belongs to Mr. S. I told him I would return it to him if I found it. Give me a couple of days to stall until I decide how to handle this."

Edna left so quickly that I didn't have time to think. My legs were weak, and I had to sit down for a minute before I could put the tiger back in the bag.

We agreed that I would check on Deacon after my shift tomorrow and decide what to do next.

The next day, Deacon seemed better. He promised me he would lay low. That second night, he seemed more himself. I sat with him after his supper, wondering if I needed to talk about the bag in my closet. He pulled an old metal chair and the remnants of a hay bale out near the edge of the swamp.

"Wanna light a fire?"

"Sure, Deacon, but keep it real low."

He pulled some dried sticks, empty boxes, and branches together, piled real neat on a bare piece of ground. Then he bent to light the pile and blow on the tiny flame. Once the fire got going, Deacon thought of Preacher.

"When we built a fire over yonder, we'd watch to be sure it didn't get too big. Sometimes we'd use old boxes and newspapers or rotted wood for our fires." He held his lips together tight.

"That Preacher, he was a talker. He had a lot in his head, you know. He could name stuff off like a preacher. "

I nodded my head. "Really, like what?"

"You know, stuff, like the books of the Bible. I liked to hear him say Leviticuz, Exoduz, and Lamenta-tations."

Deacon's face lit up. "And the twelve apostles, the eight dwarfs, and all of Santa's reindeer."

The more excited he got, the more he would stutter. "And, and, uh, and the states and their capitals, too. He learned that in fifth grade under Miss McClary."

Deacon squinted his eyes. "Tallahaaassee, Shy-ann, Mount Peel-e-ar. Then sometimes he'd recite poems he learned under Miss Higgs."

Deacon stood and dragged a piece of wood from the hedge onto the fire. The embers shot sparks up in the dark sky. He squatted by the fire to warm his hands.

Deacon stared into the fire, and so did I.

"Sometimes all I could hear was the hum of his voice and feel the fire come and go when he moved around and stood between it and me."

I didn't say anything. The wood fell, and the fire jumped with blue and yellow flames as the red embers glowed.

"But one of my favorites was the tiger poem . ."

Deacon stopped for a minute and took a deep breath. "Tyger, Tyger, burning bright in the forests of the night,

What immortal hand or eye

Could frame the scary skin or hide."

He peered at me and then back at the fire. "I'd pat my hand on my leg like this, and he'd say the words, "And, when my heart began to beat, What dread hand? And what dread feet?"

Deacon swayed from side to side with the words in perfect time with the beat, patting his foot, beating out the words with his hand against his thigh, his big head nodding. Those words and the fire recalled that time with his only friend.

His voice grew a little louder. "What the hammer? What the chain? In what furnace was your brain?"

He rolled his big head back and around, then said, "Some nights he'd say the whole poem, and some nights he'd forget."

Deacon shook his head. "He knew it was one of my favorites. That's why when we found the tiger, he let me keep it. 'Cause I liked that poem, and I weren't scared of the wampus when I had it."

I hated to interrupt. "Deacon, you know that there's no wampus cat around here."

"Oh, Missy, I heared it howling out by the river lots of times."

"I think that might be some other creature."

"No, ma'am. Me and Preacher both heard hit. That's why we'd keep the fires going. To skeer her off. That's what we do, you know."

Deacon squatted for a moment, staring at the fire and pitching sticks into it slowly. Then he levered himself to his feet, slowly due to his stiffness and bruises, and paced. His shadow was thrown against the barn wall. His eyes stared at the fire. His big hand patted the side of his leg again as he paced and repeated those lines. "When the stars threw down their spears, And water'd heaven with their tears."

Then Deacon raised his hand, as big as a catcher's mitt, high above his head like a preacher exhorting the sinners and said: "Did He smile His work to see? Did He who made the lamb make me?"

Deacon gazed upward for who knows what. His arm fell back to his side. Then he was silent—silhouetted there in the moonlight.

I gazed into the fire. All I could see now was that sleek tiger formed by Bugatti's hands, still alive today, hiding in my closet, power and beauty captured like that poem forever. Deacon and Preacher had felt its power, too. They had no idea of the Bugatti's value. They wanted what they felt in the tiger.

Was that creature all evil then, or was there some good in the tiger and Preacher and all the rest of us so-called mortals?

Deacon's eyes were glazed. He hung his head. After a few minutes, he stared beyond the fire into the woods.

"But I dunno what I done with it. Maybe that's okay. Maybe it's out there somewhere protecting you, Missy."

I nodded. I didn't need to say anything right then to Deacon. I didn't want to disturb his memories.

"Watch this fire now, and then you better turn in, Deacon."

"Yassum."

As I walked back from the swamp's edge, I tried to cross the last two blocks quickly, but I stopped when the clock chimed. As I stood there counting the gongs, my breathing slowed down. I could smell something. I looked for a mimosa tree with its sweet, pink blossoms or some honeysuckle somewhere. I didn't see either one. The clock struck its final chime.

Then I spied a cluster of white flowers spiraling down the rain gutter on the deserted blacksmith shop. I walked over and bent one near to me. Moonflowers. It must be. Even as I stood there, another one began to open slowly. The moonflower was as big as Deacon's gnarled hand, reaching up toward the moon, big and powerful but seeking. The round, moon-shaped petals were as strikingly white as the moon itself. The hypnotic, powerful scent covered me. I could only stand and stare. Moonflowers. The darkness opened them. The moon and Madam's moonflowers were there all over Paradise Alley.

The next day, I walked down to Paradise Alley after lunch. Not much was stirring. I called Deacon's name, but he didn't answer. I swung the door open and walked back to the corner where the cot was. He was gone. The cot was straightened as if he hadn't slept there the night before. He must have left last night after I had.

Edna didn't call Mr. S right away. He and Lydia were out of town. Edna said she was trying to figure out how to handle this. I wanted her to go ahead and take the tiger over to the gallery at least, but for some reason, she said no.

Those lines that Deacon sounded for me haunted me at night. His big hand patting out the rhythm, repeating the words his friend would say. Reaching for the stars and moonlight and God knows what else. That tiger was his talisman, his protection. But not Preacher's. Could evil win the battle disguised as a protector? The Bugatti tiger stayed tucked away in that filthy Crown Royal bag in my closet.

At first, I checked on that beautiful cat frequently to see if it was still there. Then I decided to leave the cat alone, safe enough in my closet. Besides, Edna knew where the tiger hid its power in the dark. One thing I knew for sure; Mr. S would not rest until he had the tiger.

30

Edna, Rico, and Danger

I couldn't wait any longer. I called Edna and told her to come by my apartment that night after supper. I needed to get some things straight.

She called my name from the bottom of the stairs.

"Yoohoo, Mesha, anybody home?"

I leaned over the railing. "Come on up, Edna."

She huffed and puffed, but determined as she was, she arrived at the top with a grin that she'd won. We settled around the kitchen table.

"Look, Edna, we need to figure out what we're gonna do. This is getting serious, and somebody else is gonna get hurt. I'd just as soon it not be me."

Edna nodded as she surveyed my apartment, pausing to think. "I guess now's as good a time as any. Got anything to drink besides coffee up here?"

I obliged and dug out the bottle of gin hidden in the cabinet's back corner. We sat down with the bottle between us and our glasses half-filled with ice and lemonade. I was sure both of us were thinking about that tiger lurking in my closet.

Edna began, "Remember last winter when I was going through some things? I went to Memphis and kind of hinted to you later that I met somebody?"

"Yes, if I remember right, you came back purring like an alley cat."

"Well, as I said, I met somebody, but my frolic didn't turn out like I expected," she said. "I didn't want to get you involved, but I am gonna need your help."

"That's what I'm here for."

Edna stared past me for a moment. Her lips squeezed together in a grimace. She shook her head slightly.

"I met this guy. I thought at the time it was just a fling maybe. The first time I met him, he was smooth, and I fell for it." She paused. "His name is Rico."

"Whoa. Wait a minute now; tell me exactly what happened."

We took a sip of our gin fizzes. She had waited for me to ask. I think she realized she needed to tell her story out loud.

Edna began talking, and I listened. "You remember I was going stir crazy? I needed to get out of Nuanz and see the world. The manager of the Peabody Hotel in Memphis is the son of Mildred Landry, who ran a dress shop here. I helped Mildred when she was a young widow, and times were hard. She told me countless times that her son, Quadrille, kept an extra room available for her. Anytime I want to use it, just call. I get a big discount. I like to let people pay me back if it's possible." She winked.

"My first trip a few months ago to Memphis was to be a short getaway. My body hates the winter more each year. I've been thinking about moving to Florida. I planned to visit a few places and kind of imagine what it would be like to live there. I was ready to try something new. Nobody knows who Edna Love is in big ole Memphis. I needed a few days of that."

She paused and closed her eyes briefly as she thought back. I sat as she told her story.

A Few Months Ago

Edna said she checked into the Peabody Hotel downtown on the river. She registered and unloaded her luggage, then ventured out onto Poplar Avenue. People were everywhere. Traffic was backed up. A roaming guitar player was on the corner with his case out to take donations. She added her name to the wait list at the Rib Shack, and she sipped her tequila sunrise as she waited for her name to be called.

The waiter asked if Edna would like another drink, and she said, "Why not?" All she had to remember was which way the river was.

The ribs and tiny paper cup of slaw were delicious with the warm loaves of bread. She had another drink with dinner, but she felt sane right then. She gazed across the crowd and into the face of a man sitting alone with his back against the wall. He was giving her the once-over. She held his stare, picked up her drink, and peered at him over the glass. He finally nodded his head. He looked familiar. Maybe she had seen him in Memphis before. But she couldn't place him.

The waiter appeared, and she asked for the check. When the check arrived, she added a generous tip and left. She made herself not look in the man's direction and climbed the steep staircase from the Rib Shack. Poplar Avenue was crowded, and she strolled toward the Peabody Hotel. Not too fast, not too slow. Couples sauntered along, mainly young ones but a few older couples. She seemed to be the only single woman over thirty here at this time of night—dark thirty.

She pushed open the door to the Peabody Hotel lobby, quieter but filled with people and beautiful, upholstered settees, chairs, and mahogany end tables. She sat down where she could watch the door and the people without being too obvious. After a few minutes, the stranger from the Rib Shack came in the door. He didn't see her, and she edged behind the palmetto palm a little more. An older woman with a Pekingese dog under her arm came in, glancing around to see if anyone had noticed her entrance. Then a middle-aged couple came in. He led the way, and she walked a step or two behind.

Suddenly, a waiter appeared with a drink on a tray and laid a coaster on the table next to her.

"The gentleman sent over an after-dinner drink." He set a Black Russian on the coaster, straightened, and smiled.

Edna was flustered. "I really don't think this is for me."

"Oh, yes, he pointed you out," the waiter said. "The lady beside the palm in the red dress."

He smiled and shrugged his shoulders. "I think that would be you."

"Thank you," she said as she reached for her purse.

"He's taken care of it all."

She nodded. She leaned back in her chair as she lifted the glass to her lips. She wondered if he was going to appear. The drink was perfect. Like a dessert that carried the spicy barbecue taste away and said, "Relax, Edna. You've got this."

She expected him to round the corner, but she drank her Russian slowly and people-watched. No one appeared. After another half hour at least, she was ready to find her room. She pushed out of the chair. Surely, he had grown tired of waiting for this old dame to totter toward the door, but she expected some kind of interruption. She walked to the elevator, and as the door slid open, the attendant asked, "What floor?"

Behind her, the stranger said, "I hope you have a good night."

And there he was. The elevator man held his hand against the open door and raised his eyebrows at her.

"Thank you for the drink."

The stranger tilted his head. "I didn't want to ruin your night, but I couldn't resist."

"You didn't ruin it exactly. Just surprised me, I guess."

There was a moment of space and time, shadowy. He had his back to the lobby lights. The man looked more familiar now that he was closer. He was older than she'd thought. His dark hair had a few streaks of gray, and there were lines around his eyes and on his cheeks. He waited expectantly.

"I was about to call it a night," Edna said.

"Would you like to see the river before you go?"

Edna felt a little jolt jump in her spine. Then she waved the elevator man on. The doors closed, and she turned to the stranger. They walked toward the hotel parking lot.

Edna said, "You know, I probably have a nice .22 derringer inside this big purse."

He threw back his head and laughed, musical like a flourish of hands on a piano.

He said, "I wouldn't doubt that one bit."

"I am Rico . . ." He stopped and studied her face. "Rico Martes."

"I am Edna Love."

He said, "I am not trying to swindle you or trick you. I just want to show you the river and maybe a few stars above it."

"There's nothing wrong with that, now is there?" Edna said.

They walked down two blocks. The street took a sharp downward turn. They talked the way two adult strangers meeting for the first time would talk. She tried not to reveal too much and enjoyed being beside a good-looking man who could walk without falling down. He wasn't overly curious, just polite. They approached the riverwalk easily. There lay the Mighty Mississippi. She hadn't taken the time to stop and gaze at the river for a while. There wasn't much to see in the dark, but you could feel the river. Its power, its strength.

They stopped at a bench there, and he pointed at a barge coming down the river. "That one is probably from Cape Girardeau on its way to New Orleans, maybe with a stop at Vicksburg."

"I haven't seen a barge in a long time. That looks like a big load."

"Yes, this time of year, it could be grain or cotton bales even that have been in storage."

The waves lapped against the banks. The lights on the barge were red and green.

"Look, there's another one behind it."

"I know a guy that works on a riverboat. Wonder if Joe is on that one?" Edna said.

Rico didn't say a word. The breeze picked up and played with her silk shawl. But it felt good, and she was surprised that she was so comfortable with this stranger.

"Well, we saw the river; now let's look at the moon," he said.

He caught Edna's elbow and steered her down the walkway, his touch giving her a little zing. There were plenty of people around. At the end of the walkway, they took the sloping walk, and he pointed to a secluded place. There was a hedge and an arch with a sign she couldn't read in the dimness. They met two couples chattering and laughing. She walked on with Rico, and then as the path turned and climbed a bit, suddenly there was a wooden platform with others huddled there. He told her quietly that this was an old lookout that few people knew about. She stumbled on a board and stubbed her toe. He caught her with one hand on her arm, the other encircling her back.

He led her over to the side and said, "Look up."

There was the moon, of course. Clear and bright with a few wispy clouds, a moon larger and brighter than she remembered. She could feel the river near them. The city lights were obscured behind the trees. She stared at that white glow for a moment.

Then Rico said, "And there's the North Star."

He pointed back over her shoulder. "Find the Big Dipper; then follow those three stacked stars." His finger drew an imaginary line that dipped, then slanted up a bit. She saw the North Star, a bright blue, and suddenly she felt a little ripple of pleasure.

"Oh my. I wasn't expecting this in downtown Memphis." She turned and thanked him.

He leaned on his elbows. "There's something about the moon and the river together. It's powerful, isn't it?"

She arranged to meet Rico again for a weekend in Memphis, and this time it turned out to be more of what she had expected. They ended up in a suite at the Peabody, which became their place. She would sneak out every chance she could get to meet him.

Edna and Rico started making plans, like there was a future somewhere. He was reserved, entertaining, and smart. But something about him kept tickling her brain.

His dark eyes entranced her the most. They enticed her. Delight or dread, she didn't know. Her head told her to be careful. Her heart said to jump in with both feet. *Last chance, Edna,* she thought.

It was like she had shed a couple of decades of living when she was with Rico. He made her feel young again. He always said the right thing.

Edna couldn't help herself. She wanted this man and everything that his eyes seemed to promise.

One weekend, she asked him, "Rico. Tell me. What gets you up in the morning?"

"Edna, you know. People, money, desire. I am a gambler. I like to push things to the edge. Drive up the stakes. If there's a problem, fix it."

"Are you on your own?" Edna asked.

"To some degree. But I have been with this boss for over twenty years."

"Really? Who is he?" She wanted to get a name if she could.

"You wouldn't know him," Rico said. "He's been in another part of the country for generations."

"He must respect you," Edna observed.

"Always. That's why I keep working for him."

"What exactly do you do for this guy?"

Rico smiled. "I help him make money. Lots of it."

"How much of it is legit?"

He laughed. "Edna, darling. Not 100 percent, but close. That's one of the reasons I am here."

He reached over and touched her cheek.

Then he said, "Do you ever wish you could go back and change some things?"

"Who doesn't do that?" Edna answered.

"Do you think it's possible?" he asked.

"Depends," Edna said.

"Yeah, I guess it does," he smiled.

Rico and Edna met up every ten days or so. Sunday was her driving day to get there. Tuesday was her day to come back by five o'clock. Once she got that established, she could slip away and know everything was taken care of.

She kept telling herself to go easy. He had all the right answers all the time. She felt she was running blind through a snowstorm, and all she could think was she was glad she brought her coat.

She kept the last receipt from The Peabody. She paid for their room the last time.

Sitting in the Moonlight in Meshac's Apartment

"I know you must think I'm crazy to remember all of this, but I do. I would go over every word and phrase, trying to plant them in my brain. Then later, I tried to figure things out," Edna said.

Edna got up and walked over to the window of my apartment. I watched her. Waiting. The clock began chiming, and we counted the chimes and smiled. It became quiet again.

"One conversation we had lodged permanently. I went over it in my head many times. Look here, I wrote some down in your little book of secrets you gave me."

Edna laid her book of secrets on the table.

I didn't move. I didn't want to stop this outpouring.

Edna looked me in the eye.

"I should have known something was strange when he asked me, 'Do you ever wish you could go back and change some things?'"

Edna shook her finger. "That conversation should have told me a lot. But I was too damn busy being Miss Oh-I-Am-So-Happy and my life is getting better that I took no notice at all."

She leaned over with her hands on the table and looked at me.

"Until Preacher was killed . . . and I saw something with my own two eyes. That was when I pieced things together."

We sat there. I didn't know what to do next. Edna Love had been duped by a fast-talking son of a bitch.

Edna added, "But I played along, and now all of this is on my head. Not only have I ruined my life but the life of Nuanz. They did nothing to deserve this. Nothing at all but be nice to a dumb, old, bossy broad."

"What do you mean? How is this hurting us?"

"Mesha, haven't you noticed how there's a rough crowd coming in for those auctions? Strange men driving out-of-state cars for no reason?"

She shook her head. "And the cops? They're not studying Mr. S. He's making donations to their retirement fund. Trust me, he is. Even the mayor and those old men on the city board. They're getting ready to let Mr. S open a club right next to the Depot. He's turning them against me—he is. He's flashing money all over the place. Told them I've not been keeping my place open, and he can do better."

Edna sighed, and I waited.

"I don't get this. You've lost me now. Go on," I said.

She thumbed through the book.

She continued, "So back in early spring, what happened is Rico and I met up about every ten days. I drove on Sundays to get there and tried to come home by Tuesday at five o'clock. I figured that way nobody would know I was slipping off, and everything here would be okay.

"I knew I needed to be careful, but even knowing that, I listened to his honey-sweet lies and sopped them up like dessert. I guess I was love blind. My mama would've reminded me there is a sucker born every minute."

I wanted to pat Edna's hand, but I knew that would be the wrong response.

Her voice trembled a little. "He was so clever and so slick. I never would have figured it out until it was too late. At least, they thought it was too late."

Then I saw it in her eyes. I could name it because I knew it well—revenge.

Edna's voice dripped with sarcasm, "Poor Rico. Poor, little, pitiful Rico Martes."

"Oh my God. Are you sure?"

She nodded her head and gave me the look.

Her words tumbled out: "When I saw him come in the lobby midmorning that Sunday after the big auction, I figured he was as eager as I to be there—with me. He had no reason to look for me—not this early. I took a moment to study him standing alone, objectively if I could. His eyes narrowed as he scanned the crowd. He held his arms folded tightly around his body. I stepped back out of his sight and looked to see what he was seeing. There were several groups of people. Some arriving; some leaving.

"There were two men dressed in suits and ties and three glittering young women with them. Rico walked their way as the circle opened to include him. They all knew each other. I stayed where I was. Suddenly, a voice drifted above the others in the lobby. The men turned toward the doorway, and another man approached them. Rico's back was to me. Then as the room cleared, I saw the man approaching them. His hair combed back. His face wreathed in a smile. It was Guido Salvatorre and Lydia was with him. Rico stepped away from the group and patted Guido's back as they hugged. They were enveloped into the circle."

Edna patted her chest. "Rico—my Rico—nodded his head and bent forward to listen to Guido. Then I heard Lydia's voice clear as a bell.

"Oh, Freddie, I have missed you so. Dear, sweet Freddie."

Edna's eyes teared up. "I hesitated only an instant. I walked out the back entrance and down the street through the parking lot as fast as I could. I ducked into a coffee shop and dived into a booth there. When they brought me a coffee, I could not even lift it to my mouth, I was shaking so hard. Part of me wanted to deny what I had seen. To make it make sense. While at the same time, I was ready to throw up. My face must have been red. The waitress said, 'Are you all right?' I could only shake my head and think, 'So what are you gonna do, Edna Love? You fool. What are you gonna do now?'"

Edna's face was white. She stared out the window as she continued. "They hugged and laughed, and I—I ran to my car. I drove across the river and sat on a bed in a little run-down motel in Arkansas and cried and cried. I stayed there huddled up for days, not wanting to live. Not wanting to come back to Nuanz and face everybody."

I whispered. "That's when you showed up at the Bluebird Cafe looking like hell."

She didn't answer. We sat there, huddled around the table. Finally, I asked, "You're sure now it's Freddie?"

I hesitated, then blurted out, "You think he might have killed Preacher? Trying to find the Bugatti?"

I looked at those chopsticks in her hair instead of her face.

"And now they're trying to close down the Oasis? Oh, my, Edna."

I didn't know what to say, but I knew I had to say something. I took a deep breath and let the words tumble out of my mouth.

"Edna, people have terrible passages they must live through. All of us do. When that happens, sometimes we are the ones who can take the battering. Sometimes we are the ones who are ready to jump off that cliff. If we are lucky, we don't all live through the same passage at the same time.

"You know if there are enough of us who are brave, we can lean on each other and hold on until the next brave ones arrive.

"I have learned a few things about life. This place, this time, this circumstance is really only a tiny part of the universe. When you bare your soul, sometimes a cold, cruel reality sweeps in and bites you in the ass. But you know we learn from those times, too. All I can do is mutter a prayer: keep us sane, keep us safe, and, dear God, keep us going."

Edna looked at me and nodded her head.

31

A Plan

It was dead quiet. Then I heard the owl hoot twice as it coasted over the trees on the square. "Guido Salvatorre is either running stolen goods, or fakes, or a little of both here in Nuanz. Whatever, he's a criminal. So is Rico Martes," Edna said.

"I thought Deacon might help, but now he's run out on me. Can't say I blame him."

She shook her head. "I need help. There's still Madam. Can you bring her to me?"

"Geez, I don't know. I don't like to mess with Madam. I don't think she likes me."

"Tell her it's for Edna. She'll come, I promise."

"When and where?"

Edna eased back in her chair. "Rico is coming to Nuanz next Wednesday. I think he suspects something, so I need to be ready. See if she'll come by Monday night. Moose can close for me. We will begin."

I decided then that I better explain further. "I had a conversation with Gracie. She says things are not what they seem at the auction house. Two sets of invoices maybe? She wouldn't say if she thought the stuff was stolen or fakes. What do you think, Edna?"

"We know he has some expensive items there. We know that people legitimately know the good stuff and pay the high prices. So he's either substituting fakes for the good stuff or may be mingling fakes with the real thing," Edna said, considering what she knew.

"That would be a possibility. You got to have a legit name out there to get some of this stuff, I know. I don't know that much about fake paintings and stuff, but I've heard that happens a lot."

"Yeah, knowing Guido, he's got something going on, either as a cover for the real thing or hiding stolen items or drugs inside the boxes."

"Maybe that's what Preacher and Deacon were looking for in the house next to the lumber shed there," I said. "That's when they found the tiger."

"Strange that Guido didn't have a better handle on where the good stuff was."

"I think Lucille may be cheating on her boss every now and then."

"That's one way to look at it. So how are we gonna prove it?"

Edna narrowed her eyes. "Our only hope is Grace."

I thought, *Not again. Let's not go there.*

I asked, "Are you sure we need her?"

"Yes. We are going to need hard proof, and Grace is the closest one to the books."

I didn't argue this time. I knew she was right.

"I'll see what she can come up with that maybe they won't even notice."

"I know you can figure out something."

Meek and obedient as always, I said, "I'll try."

"Have you heard of a tiger being a good thing? Maybe he wants to help us out, too. Oh, 'Tyger, Tyger, burning bright.' Ha ha. Didn't know I knew a poem, too, now did you?"

Edna leaned over. "Got to keep your eyes wide open all of the time, Mesha."

She nodded her head and straightened those beautiful chopsticks.

"Now, I am picking up my fat self and battling on."

32

Oasis on Fire

The Oasis was on fire. When I heard the sirens go by about three in the morning, they sounded close, but I couldn't really tell. I couldn't go back to sleep. I got up when I smelled smoke, and I got dressed to be sure everything was okay downstairs.

When I stepped out onto the sidewalk, a heavy fog was settling over downtown. After I knew the Bluebird was okay, I walked to the corner and saw the smoke billowing from Depot Street. At first, I thought it was the old, vacant train depot. Then someone came by and hollered, "It's the Oasis. She's on fire."

I didn't know what to do, but I walked to the next block. The police had everything blocked off. There were two fire trucks with hoses snaked all over the place. The owner of the gas station a block away was shutting off his tanks. The fire was still involved.

I spotted Mr. Rogers and asked him if the building was lost. "Don't know for sure yet. Lots of smoke, and they broke out a couple of windows to get more water in there."

We stood there for a minute. "The guys down at The Grill called it in as they were locking up. Otherwise, the Oasis would have been totaled probably."

He looked at me. "Nobody knows where Edna is."

I shook my head. "I have no idea."

"Well, there's something funny going on."

I stared at the smoke-filled block and climbed the hill. Fire is a scary thing. This might be what wound it up for Edna and Nuanz. If it was deliberately set, then what kind of message was that? I knew the cafe would be buzzing all day.

There was another body. This one was found in the alley between the Oasis and the body shop. Nobody knew who it was. He didn't have any ID on him, and Edna Love wasn't around to help identify him. Moose didn't want to get involved. They couldn't figure out if the dead guy was the one who set the fire, or if he passed out and was overcome by the smoke. The medical examiner would have to figure that out, so they said. "They said" was all the information we were getting. I hoped it wasn't Johnny.

33

Bluebird Buzzing

As usually happens when something's going on, everybody piled into the cafe. The Bluebird was buzzing. The Liars' Table was so loud that I didn't even have to pretend I was checking their refills. I could hear them all the way at the front counter. Miss Lewis turned once or twice at the Ladies' Table to glare them down to some level of normal talk, but they never noticed. When I eased over to check on the ladies, she addressed me. "Mesha, can you get them to calm down?"

"I doubt it. You know how they feel about Edna."

"Yes, I know. We are concerned, too, but I can't hear myself think."

Then Mary Craig piped up. "Mesha, have you heard anything official about the man they found?"

"No, ma'am. I kept thinking the sheriff might stop by, but I guess he's busy right now."

"I am sure he is."

About that time, the door opened, and the skinny, scary man came in. It was one of those moments that everything gets quiet. Of course, he was so skittish anyway, I figured he might just hightail it out of there.

I leaned over and said to the women, "Keep talking. Keep it normal."

They immediately began chattering, and the quietness disappeared, but of course, people were sneaking looks at the man.

I sauntered over to the lunch counter and asked, "Would you like a cup of coffee?"

He nodded and slid onto the end stool.

I poured his coffee quickly and asked if he wanted to see a menu. He didn't answer me. His hand shook when he brought the cup to his mouth. He swallowed two big gulps as if the coffee wasn't even warm.

I kept standing there, waiting.

"Have you seen Miss Edna?"

"No, sir."

'That was her place that burned last night, wasn't it?"

His clothes reeked of smoke. Maybe he stood around and watched the fire. Maybe not.

"Yes, sir. The Oasis belongs to Edna Love. But she hasn't been around here for a few days now."

He nodded his head and then remembered the cup in his hand. He blew on the coffee this time and took a quick sip.

I couldn't help myself from asking, "Do you know Edna?"

"I did a long time ago. She don't remember me, though."

"What's your name?"

"My name don't matter. I just, uh, I just owe Edna."

He gazed out the front window, then turned back to me. "Looks like I am too late."

"It's never too late with Edna Love. Trust me."

We sat for a moment, and the other quiet voices calmed him and softened his grip. I prayed no one would decide to approach us and break this instant in time.

I tried not to look directly at him. "Is there anything I can do?" I pretended to straighten the stack of menus.

He folded his arms on the counter and hung his head. "I need to find Edna."

"Well, there are several who need to find her. Where are you staying?"

He looked at me. "Around. Been sleeping in the depot the last few nights."

I leaned a little closer. "Did you see anything last night? About the fire?" I asked.

"Not exactly. I had walked up to Edna's house and was hid out there hoping she'd come in. I fell asleep, and then the sirens woke me up. By the time I got down there, everything was roped off. But I been watching."

About then, Mr. White got up to come pay his bill. I said, "Hang on," and went to the register.

Several more stragglers came to check out. When I turned around, the man looked like he was ready to bolt.

"Step out here on the sidewalk with me for a minute." He nodded his head and followed me.

"Look, I can get you in to see Edna, but she needs to at least know your name."

He gazed over the square, his eyes sad. "Tell her it's Harold from a long time ago."

I nodded my head. "I'll see if I can get us together at her house tonight. Say around nine o'clock?"

He nodded his head.

"Just knock on her back door. I'll be there."

I hoped he would show up.

Part V
The Payback

Edna's Revenge Begins

The crowd lingered, and a few others joined us. People marked time, for what, I didn't know. But suddenly, Edna appeared at the front door of the Bluebird. I thought at first she was going to cry.

"Edna." I went to hug her, but she stuck her arms out and shoved me to the side. The cafe wasn't full, but there were several tables of people. We stared at her, and then she stepped in a pace or two. She opened her mouth, but nothing came out at first. I stood there, shocked, like everyone else waiting.

"I want everybody to know that I am back, and I am going to find out who in the hell has dared to do this to me."

She staggered a little, and her eyebrows pinched together. "Fair warning to you fine citizens of Nuanz. I want names. I want answers. I will not hold back until I find the SOB who did this to me. If you're sitting here in this room right now, just know that payback is hell."

The ventilator fan in the kitchen whirred in the quiet. I didn't know what to do but stand there with my mouth hanging open. She turned and threw open the door so hard the bells jangled like a brass band. She was gone before anyone, including myself, could say a word.

Wow, I thought. *That was quite a performance, Edna.* 'Cause she knew, or thought she knew, who had done it, and they weren't sitting at the Bluebird's tables. Maybe that would give us some time to deal with those who had.

When I got off work that night, I walked to Edna's house, hoping she would let me in and that Harold would show. Her Caddy was in the driveway, but there were no lights on. I hollered through the door, "Edna, it's me. Need to talk to you."

Nothing. Not a sound. "Come on, Edna. Let me in."

I waited a few more minutes. I hated to go peeping in the windows. I had about decided to walk back to the square when I thought I heard her footsteps. Finally, I saw the top of her head as she made her way to the door. She cracked it open. "Is it just you?"

"Of course. Let me in."

She eased the door back, and I squeezed in. She shut the door and locked it immediately. The house was dark. I could barely see where to walk. She started back to the den. Silence. No chatter. We stood in the middle of the room, and she looked at me like she didn't even know who I was.

"Edna, what can I do? Are you okay?"

She stared right through me. "What do you think?"

"Have you talked to the sheriff?" She nodded her head.

"So what? Do they know anything?"

She shook her head no. "Do you really think our police force can figure out what happened?"

"Surely they'll call in the state fire marshal."

"I don't want any more people snooping around in my business than I have to have."

"How bad is it?"

"The fire department broke all the windows, and water is everywhere. But the walls are still standing."

She came to herself and sat in her chair. I sat down to listen.

"The back office is not too bad. The carpet is ruined and all the furniture, but my important papers were locked in the safe. There were some accounting books on my desk, but I can piece that together. They won't let me get in there and start clearing out until they know more."

"Was it arson?"

"I have no doubt. The Oasis hadn't even been opened for a week. Moose closed it down last Saturday night and decided to wait until he heard from me to reopen."

I decided now was not the time to interrogate Edna about where she was when the place caught on fire, but obviously, someone knew where she was because she heard about the fire and came home.

"Who are your best suspects?"

She gave me that look. "I have a very long list, but I am zeroing in on two. "

I waited for more. "Want to share that with me?"

"Not at this time." She looked away so I couldn't read her eyes.

"Edna, you know I am here for you anytime."

She looked at me then. "Yes, I know that, kid."

Her voice was soft and sad.

"If you need me to ride shotgun on some vigilante wild ride again, I will be there."

She did smile, but that was all I could get out of her. Then there was a knock on the back door. I hoped it was Harold.

"Who is that?" Edna's eyes got big.

"I bet it's that guy from auction night. The one who's been trying to see you."

I went to the door and looked out. Sure enough, it was him.

"It's the skinny guy we all have been avoiding. His name is Harold. He said to tell you from 'long ago,' whatever that means. He might could help us out. He said he really needs to talk to you."

Edna said, "Let him in."

We sat down in Edna's den. She didn't offer us any refreshments.

"So, Harold, at last, we meet." Edna's voice was cold. Her eyes glinted with that hardness she carried within her.

"I been trying to see you for some time, Miss Edna."

"Let's see, you're Harold Bingham? Is that right?"

Harold dropped his head. "Yes, ma'am."

"I remember you now. That was a long time ago."

"Yes, it was."

"Well, what is it you've been trying to tell me, Harold? Sit down."

He sat on the chair's edge, looking pale, and his shoulders stooped forward as if he was ashamed somehow. His baseball cap was crumpled in his hands.

Edna looked at him. "I can save you some time. I know about Freddie Garcia. Don't know exactly why he chose to come back here, but I know who he is. What I need to know is why."

"Yes, ma'am." His voice was low. He spoke quickly.

"I know Freddie took something from you and disappeared with that girl, Annabel? Remember that fall I got in some big trouble, and you helped me out on that drug bust thing? Put me on the bus out of town . . ." He glanced at Edna. She didn't say anything, just waited for him to go on.

"I made it pretty good for a while, then fell back into drugging."

The words hung there like a black, oily smudge. But there was no time for clucking our tongues or shaking our heads. Harold looked everywhere but at Edna. Then he crossed his leg and his foot started jiggling.

"I was down on my luck, living in Nashville, and Freddie Garcia recognized me there on a street corner begging for money. He offered me a job with Mr. S. I had to take it. I needed a place to hide. There was men looking for me by then." He looked straight at Edna. "Didn't he look familiar to you, Miss Edna? I thought you'd figure it out."

Edna reached for a little glass heart that lay on the table beside her chair. She turned it over in her hands and propped it against the photograph there. After a long moment, she said, "Harold, I had no idea. I mean, I didn't even recognize you at first."

"I know. Hit's been a long time." He waited, still not able to look at

Edna directly. The silence lay over us. Then Harold uncrossed his leg. With both feet on the floor, he leaned forward a bit.

"When me and Freddie talked about the past, we'd always come around to Nuanz. People we both knew. What went on here and stuff like that. Then Mr. S got in some hot water worse than usual. He was going big guns—some legal, some not, but his name was tossed around in the big cities. He needed to tamp it down some. The authorities was watching us. So that's when Freddie come up with the idea—why not hide in the wide open? Freddie said he knew a little town not far from Memphis that'd be a perfect hiding place."

Edna looked at me. I stayed silent. Harold wanted to set it all out.

He cleared his throat. "Freddie talked about you a lot. I knowed they was going after you, too. They thought you'd fall right over and do whatever they asked with the right threat. I hoped they wouldn't hurt you, but then ..." His eyes turned down to the corner of the room. "Then I knowed it was gonna be you or them. I couldn't let that happen."

He lifted tired, sad eyes to Edna. "I knowed I had to try. I owed you, Miss Edna."

"So they thought they could run me out of town? Or worse? Why?"

"Well, uh, they thought they might could get you to help them be accepted, trusted like, and then if you wanted a cut, they would make you an offer. But something changed. After Preacher and the tiger and all. I reckon that's why Mr. S called in more of his guys."

"Mr. S ordered the hit on Preacher?"

"Yessum."

"Did they set fire to the Oasis?"

Harold nodded his head.

"I figured as much."

We all sat there. "Are you gonna be okay, Harold?"

"I don't know. I'm gonna figure something out."

"Well, thank you, Harold. I hope things work out for you."

He gazed sadly at Edna and pushed his way to his feet, like an old man. I walked down the hall with him to unlock the door. He whispered to me, "Use this if you have to" as he thrust a folded piece of paper in my hand and squeezed out the side door.

I didn't open the paper until I got back to the office with Edna. She leaned her head against the cushion and stared at the ceiling. I laid the paper on the desk next to the glass heart.

She picked it up and read the rough print aloud:

"Call FBI Special Agent Marcus Sanders in New York City. He hunts stolen art."

We both sat there for a minute. It was hard to take it all in.

"Let's have a big powwow and see if we can't figure this out," I said to Edna.

"I'll get Madam to come to your house on Monday. That will give us a couple of days to see how we can handle Rico or Freddie or whatever his name is."

"Well, we better hurry. He's catching on fast. That's obvious since they burned the Oasis."

"Do you think Sheriff Hensley is involved, too?"

"Willard and I go way back. I wouldn't think so. But you never know. Money does talk."

Edna shook her head. "If I have to throw a hissy fit in front of all of Nuanz, then you know I will, Mesha."

"Yes, Edna, I know you will. Once we have a plan, just try and go by it. Okay?"

"I will try, but I'm not promising anything."

"Fair enough."

She picked up the crystal-shaped heart again and held it in the palm of her hand. "Sheesh. If my daddy could see me now." She shook her head.

"Why did Freddie have to come back? Why didn't he just keep going?"

"Come on now. Let's figure this out."

"All I can figure out is I have lost. Guido and his money have won. The only thing I can hold over his head is the tiger. That might not work, either. It's worth a lot, but staying here and selling more stuff is worth more to him."

"Do you really think Nuanz is gonna abandon you?"

"Yes, I do."

"I don't. Everybody in Nuanz has been just as excited about the money Salvatorre was bringing in. Look, let me do some snooping. You try and hang on until we figure this out, okay? Tell me again about seeing Rico at the Peabody with Lydia and Mr. S."

"What is there to tell?"

"Are you sure they didn't see you?"

"Pretty sure. I was so shocked, but I knew Rico wasn't expecting me that early."

"Did he ask where you were and why you didn't appear that Sunday?"

"I don't remember. We had an understanding if one of us didn't show to let it go. He didn't like to be kept on too close a leash. I respected that. When I finally met with him again, I think I pleaded a sudden illness. Of course, Mr. S wasn't here to follow up on me anyway. So maybe it's all okay."

"You don't think they saw you at the Peabody that Sunday morning?"

"No. If they had, somebody would have come after me by now."

"We still need to move fast. Harold's mystery note here means he's going to disappear. So we don't have him to talk to the law. Mr. S and his gang are bound to be watching to see how you respond to the Oasis fire. We have to start the ball rolling now."

She bit her lip. "Okay. I will try to do whatever you say."

"Well, that's a change," I said. She gave me a half smile.

Slowly, we put things together. I was relieved. Even if we were diving headfirst over a cliff, that beat the lousy feeling of being trampled down.

All I could do now was set things in motion and stand back and watch. But I believed in Edna Love. We had a plan. We'd try our best to beat the bastards down.

As I left, Edna said in that voice of steel, "Mesha, watch your back."

I answered, "Oh, I always do that, Edna."

35

Finding My Piece of Ground

Revenge has its way of blotting out the sun, but some eventually crawl out of its shadow.

Why, then, is revenge so sweet? Why do our hearts yearn for it so? When we are cast out, and then able to undermine those who caused it—what could be any sweeter? When I am lying there, beaten, and can taste the dirt of defeat but slowly inch my foot out and trip my enemy? What makes me do that? It's human nature to exact revenge, no matter how small. Then we revel in it. Then we regret it—sometimes.

I believed there was a reason why I ended up here in Nuanz. There was an emptiness in Edna's eyes. Her hair had lost its sheen. Grayness crept around her face. Those earrings had lost their glitter.

I must remember that in the end, all I have is me. Solitary and strong or weak as tea, but still upright *me*. I may be unrecognizable to others. I may spend my entire life paying for my choices. Maybe someone else will love me as ferociously as I have loved. I don't know. But in the end, it is just me. Right now, I can accept that.

I came here with few things. Clothes on my back, two books, one pair of shoes, a roll of money. I have acquired a little more. A bed, a rocker, a coffeepot. Aunt Flo sent me my daddy's broken watch and my mother's earrings. I lost my four-footed traveling companion, Ring, on my walk here, when she left with her real person, but now I had Henry to be my friend. I gained my own piece of ground. Whether it was this tiny apartment on the court square or that moment I stood behind the counter of the Bluebird Cafe and poured Miss Florence's cup of coffee. I was lucky enough to find Joe, or he found me.

I'm full of stubbornness that was my strength when Edd Biggs tied me to a tree and left me for dead. Every year brought its gifts—both good and bad. I like to keep those gifts portable—small enough to carry with me if I had the urge to run. It feels strange to have friends who wouldn't be with me if I ran. Nothing worth having is ever easy, is it?

Evil is everywhere. You can't hide. You can't pull the covers over your head and burrow into your tear-soaked bedclothes.

That tiger in my closet said it all. He was always out there. He may be beautiful, but he was a tiger. Instinct never goes away. Which one is gonna win? It's not who deserves to win. It's who has the grit to win. What's it gonna be, Nuanz—this? Or that?

Edna was as good as dead when she made her way back to my apartment that day. The darkness nearly won her soul. But some resurrections are still possible.

Some darkness is necessary, right? You couldn't see the moon without darkness. Both good and evil hide under its cover. No darkness, no courage. Even the moonflower blooms in the dark, releases its sweetness, and welcomes the sunlight before it withers and dies.

How would we even welcome the sun if we hadn't known the moon? Paradise couldn't exist without Hell.

I guessed I couldn't blame Mr. S for his greed and violence. It was his nature—that quest for power. The darkness in his heart ate away at any goodness. But the same was true of me and all of us. We all have that possibility within us. I had been lucky. Goodness may be hidden at times, but other times, it bobs to the surface when you least expect to see good.

Now if Grace could get me something official-looking from the auction house, maybe we could pull off something. Maybe. Edna was right, though; payback is hell.

36

Madam's Moonflowers

Close to dark, I walked down to Paradise Alley. I thought maybe nobody would be out yet. Madam's moonflowers covered most of her property.

One day last summer, I lingered over my iced tea at Rem's on my day off. Miss Florence and I had some catching up to do, and talking back and forth with her felt good. She was tall, thin, beautiful, and wisdom oozed out of her pores. She and I had led the way after Noah's death with integrating the lunch counter, at least, at the Bluebird.

On that day, I yearned for more understanding. I asked Miss Florence to tell me more about Madam Taliafarro. She didn't ask why. She quietly talked about Madam's moonflowers. Florence had told me that moonflowers only bloom at night. They are magical like that. They are the only flower I ever heard of that blooms after the sun goes down.

She said, "It's like the darkness opens 'em up for a special reason."

If you were there on Paradise Alley after sunset from mid-July to the first frost, you witnessed a sight like no one else had, she said. As the sun set and darkness eased down, the moonflowers opened their buds, one by one. They climbed over Madam's rickety back porch, the post where the dinner bell was, the washroom, the boarded-up shop, and the little tool shed right on the swamp's edge that led to Lovers Lane. Miss Florence nodded as she described the darkness and the glowing blooms. Some moonflowers even climbed the tall cottonwood tree by the river. People would come to the north side of the first block of Paradise Alley and watch the flowers open. The scent floated into the air.

Miss Florence said, "We would stop what we were doing sometime during the summer and spend a little time there. The mamas would say to the children, 'Shhh. Wait now. See them opening? Look. See that white spot on the corner there? Yes, that's it.' Then another mama would say, 'Now be quiet. Close your eyes. Take a deep breath. That's the moonflowers, my child. That right there.'"

Miss Florence smiled. "Madam's moonflowers are something else. Every time I see one, I always think—here's a bit of Paradise."

She continued, "But people don't come around like they used to. The older ones now watch TV or listen to the Cardinals on the radio. The young ones ride in cars and shoot hoops on the dirt courts by the school."

When I walked onto Madam's front porch that night, I could smell the moonflowers. They hung over the doorway's edge, and I could have stood there for a while to drink in their scent. But I was on a mission. I knocked on the screen door. No one was around that I could see. A light shone in the back of the house. God only knew what kind of greeting I might get from Madam.

At last, I saw someone walking toward the door. She opened the wooden door a crack and stood there.

"Hidey," I said in my whiny, so-very-white voice. "It's me. Meshac. Miss Florence told you I needed to talk to you?"

She stared at me.

"It's about Edna."

She grunted, then stepped back from the door. "Well, come on in."

The empty living room was dim. The furniture lined the walls, and a card table sat in the middle of the room. The single lamp that was lit had a scarf draped over the shade.

Madam reached for her Garrett snuff can. As she sat down in her rocker, she pointed her finger to a hardback chair to the right. I took that command, sat, and waited.

"Miss Edna sent you?"

I nodded my head. I didn't know if I should say, "Yes, ma'am" or not. I said nothing.

I heard a rustling above my head. The floorboards creaked. It sounded like something was creeping across the upstairs floor. Maybe it was the wind, or my nerves.

I found my voice. "Edna said you could help her."

She didn't say a word, forcing me to babble on.

"She said she needed you to come to her house."

Madam didn't say anything at first. She rocked back and forth a few times. "What has she got into now?" she asked.

Her voice was that of a young woman. Low-pitched like a contralto, smooth and cool as a fresh snow. I paused for a moment, wanting to remember that. Then she reached for her spit can again, which was not a fit with her appearance.

"Tell Miss Edna I will be there about this time tomorrow."

I thanked her. I thought she was dismissing me, so I headed toward the door.

"You're the one works at the Bluebird, right?" she asked.

This time I did say, "Yes, ma'am."

She never changed her expression, then folded her arms. "Tomorrow night."

Madam peered at me with those green eyes. My eyes skittered across her face and bounced around the dead-quiet room. I thought I was getting out without a glitch, but now my feet wouldn't move.

"Come with me."

She beckoned, and I followed her to the back porch. We walked down the steps into her backyard. There was a mound of dirt with broken shards of plates around the edge. She pointed out her herb garden inside a fence with a bottle tree and boxes of fragrant herbs. I could see her tomatoes and pole beans at the back of the lot where the sun shines all day. The watermelon and cantaloupe vines ran amok on the edges. She nodded her head toward the river.

"The crows have their own plot of Indian corn close to the river. They stay there away from people most of the time."

Madam continued the tour. "That's an iron tree. Half dead, they say, but it's still standing. There's a chicken house. I converted part of it to my drying shed. That's where I do my mixing."

We stepped closer to the mound. I saw jagged limbs poking up like shards of black glass and realized they were covered in moonflower vines. They moved as if they were growing even as we watched.

In the dark, the moonflowers began opening. Softly, she murmured, "Here's the thing. Moonlight helps the vining plants, too. They grow a few feet every night, reaching for the moon. First, the darkness appears gradually as the sun fades. That's the signal—like a prod to the moonflower."

A slight breeze ruffled my hair. A bobwhite whistled in the corner of the lot.

She continued, "The darkness and the moon do their work. That invisible force. It opens each bud like a full moon. Then it spills out its perfume."

I tried not to speak or even move, but I could feel tears rolling down my face. I knew she watched me. Then she reached and tore a length of vine with her strong hands and offered it to me to hold.

"Don't touch the flower; take a deep breath." I did. The scent lifted me off the ground. My eyes squeezed shut to try and sear that on my brain and inside me.

I heard her earrings tinkle.

"The moon flowers only in the dark. Noc, he knows the darkness, too."

Then I saw a man sitting there in the twilight. It was Mr. Taliafarro. He sat with his back to us. His chair eased back and down careful-like on its front legs. His feet were propped on the remnants of an old black stump of a tree with a lantern lit there handy.

In the quiet, the crickets sang a bit, and the frogs croaked in the ditch that runs to the river. He didn't move until Madam spoke his name.

"John." He turned and looked at us then. "This here's Meshac—friend of Miss Edna's."

He nodded, slowly moving his feet off the stump. He leaned over, resting his forearms on his legs. "I saw you at Rem's before, haven't I?"

I was surprised he recognized me, but I guess a skinny white girl at Rem's lunch counter was something you might remember.

"Yessir. Me and Miss Florence are friends. Queen and Rem, too."

Then he looked at both of us.

"Whatcha need?"

He knocked out his pipe and then reached for his tobacco sack to fill it again.

Madam said in that low, musical voice, "Edna Love may be playing her card, I think."

The lit match shone in his face as he drew on the pipe stem.

"Maybe." He dragged deep on the pipe, and the gray smoke floated.

Then Madam spoke louder. "May be time to help Miss Edna out."

Noc nodded his head but didn't say anything. Madam pushed a strand of hair back and turned toward the house. I didn't have a clue what to do.

"Have a seat," Noc said and pointed to a log turned on its end. I sat and waited.

"They say Mr. Edd Biggs came after you when that little boy drowned."

"Yessir, he did. Me and Gracie."

"But you figured it out?"

"Edna did. I just went along with what she said."

He nodded his head. "That's a good idea with Miss Edna." Then he chuckled. So did I.

"There's some things going on. I been noticing."

"Yessir, there is. Probably more than I know. But I owe Edna."

"A lotta people owe Edna."

"She's gonna need some help this time. She's mad. I don't know if that will help or hurt."

He sat there for a minute. Somewhere, a door slammed shut, and I heard some voices drift our way. "Madam will take care of her part, and I'll take care of mine."

I could have burst out crying, but I didn't. At least now I wasn't alone in this.

"I sure do appreciate that, Mr. Taliafarro." He looked at me and said, "Noc." I grinned.

When I got back to my apartment, Grace was sitting on the steps. She handed me an envelope. "The inventory list is not much, but it's official-looking. If you give this to the law, you may have to fake your way explaining how you got it."

"Are you sure no one saw you?"

"Yes. Mr. S is still gone, and Lucille never heard me when I sneaked in the chapel side. The newest shipment was there, and the inventory book was waiting on the table."

"Thank you, Grace." Maybe, just maybe, we had a chance at this. I sure hoped so.

37

Monday Night Plan

When I got to Edna's on Monday night after work, she and Madam were settled in the den. They looked comfortable with each other.

"I'm sorry I'm late. I couldn't get that last slow-poking man to finish."

Edna smiled. Madam said nothing.

"Have y'all got things figured out?" I asked.

"We sure do, hon." Edna picked up a little bottle from the table and glanced at me. "The less you know, the better off you'll be."

"Fine with me. Just tell me when, where, and how."

Madam took the bottle and tipped out three white seeds. "Moonflowers," she said, "are beautiful as they bloom so white in the night. At their heart are potent seeds."

Then she unfolded a twisted knot of paper that held a pile of dried, green powder. I leaned forward to check it out. Madam crushed the seeds a bit with her hands, then funneled the powder into the bottle and added back the three seeds. That bottle was little but heavy with intentions. No one spoke for a moment.

Now what? I thought.

"All you have to do is pour Rico's drink when the time is right."

"How will I know when the time is right?"

She pointed at a set of heavy, milky blue tumblers on a tray. Each glass had a scene painted on its side. She handed one to me. "That will be Rico's. See the chip on the base there? That's how you'll know."

"Know what?"

"Which one to pour the potion in."

I took a deep breath. I was in deep now, I knew. But I had to ask.

"What's this gonna do to him?"

Madam looked directly at me.

"The potion has some power. If you're holding back, the power will release you. People are affected in different ways. Drinking this helps a person step over the threshold into truth. But be sure no one else touches that drink but Rico."

We sat there, the three of us, and I wondered what would come of this. Once again, I was in the middle of who knows what. I couldn't back out. I hoped this worked out for the sake of us and Nuanz.

38

Wednesday Woes

All day long, I tried to stay as busy as I could and not think about the meeting that night. I had arranged to take off at about four o'clock so I could gather my wits and go over the plan again with Edna. I wanted to be there before Rico showed.

When I arrived, Edna was waiting for me, and she was dressed to kill. Ha. Ha. We went over the plan again. I would offer to fix the drinks and bring them into the parlor. Then she would either ask me to leave, which I wouldn't do, or just plunge into the whole truth-bearing drama. I was the witness who hopefully would help Rico see the light or at least keep him from harming her.

I was nervous when Rico Martes tapped on the back door. Edna's perfume was subtle, but I still caught a whiff as she walked past me to let him in. I heard their greetings, and Edna said my name. Then she brought him into the room, and I met him face to face.

He was better-looking than I thought he would be. But his eyes were wary as he shook my hand with a tentative smile. We exchanged the usual chitchat: "I've heard so much about you," etc.

Then Edna said, "Mesha, why don't you bring out the drinks? I have everything in the kitchen."

To Rico, she said, "Let's sit here where it's comfortable."

I walked into the kitchen for the tray with the glasses. As we had planned, I added just a few cubes of ice and the rest of the special mixture to the one glass. I tried to lift the glass tray. It was heavier than I thought.

Hell, I can't carry this. What if I drop it? I thought. *I've carried a thousand coffee cups at least without spilling a drop. Buck up, Mesha.*

The hall was dark, but I made it to the den and set the tray on the coffee table in front of the settee. Rico's glass was nearest to me. My fingers curled around the tray's edge, and I tried not to check for the chipped piece. My hand trembled when I picked up Rico's glass. As I sat the tumbler down, the drink quivered slightly, but it didn't spill.

No one said a word until Edna lifted her glass and smiled. "Cheers, everybody." I studied the window behind Edna's head and acted as if I took a sip. We were on the road now. No turning back from this point. Idle chitchat was never my strong suit, but I thought I held on pretty good. When Edna finished her drink, I made my planned speech.

"Well, Rico, it's good to finally meet you. But I have to get back and be sure Mr. Rob locked up the Bluebird. Edna, I'll just see myself out if that's okay."

"Sure, hon. Glad you could come by."

I grabbed my purse and said good night. I made sure to close the back door, then tiptoed back to the screened-in porch, where the door was unlatched. I could see into the den from there, and I hoped I could hear everything. If I needed to scream, I didn't know that anyone would be there to help us. Edna wasted little time to start the ball rolling.

"Rico, did you think I wouldn't ever figure out it was you?"

There was no response that I could hear. I opened the door a little wider. I could see the back of Edna's head and Rico's legs. Silence. Then I heard his voice.

"Well, Edna, at first, I was just too shocked when we met face to face. Then I kept putting off my confession. I knew you would probably kill me." His voice sounded hollow as if he was testing her.

Edna demanded, "Are you responsible for Guido coming to Nuanz?"

"Yes. But it started out as a legitimate business."

"Bullshit. He hasn't been legit ever."

"Some of us try to make up for our sordid past."

"Really? How's that working out?"

He hesitated a moment. "It was going pretty good. Till Harold got cold feet."

"Thank God for Harold. He was one of my early makeover projects. I never knew what happened to him."

Rico crossed his legs and leaned forward. "Seems he had a change of heart and wanted to undo some of the bad karma."

"We will see how the karma thing works out, won't we?"

He stopped talking and leaned closer. I could see his head outlined against the darkness.

Edna stood up. "I need a large payback if you want me to keep you and Guido out of jail."

"What are you talking about?"

Edna held the invoice from Salvatorre Antique Gallery and Auction stamped with his seal. Rico studied it.

"So what's this?"

"It's proof that there were two sets of books. The value was tripled maybe? Looks like there's some fakes or stolen property. Who knows? Where do I begin?"

Edna took the invoice back to her desk. She picked up the crystal heart for a moment, placing it on top of the papers.

"How large a payback?" said Rico, dropping his act and becoming Freddie.

"I don't know if that is even possible. I am still thinking."

"Guido wants to meet with you. Maybe in Memphis?"

"I will think about it."

"What now?"

He jiggled the change in his pocket, and I could hear his foot tapping on the floor.

Here was an apology maybe. I leaned in to make sure that I wouldn't miss a word.

Freddie said, "I know I shouldn't have done a lot of things, but I can't make enough excuses. I was young, ignorant, and desperate, all those years ago."

Edna rose a little on those high heels of hers.

"And what are you now, Freddie? Older, wiser, or crueler, and hardened? You left me and my mother nearly destitute when you cleaned out our cash. After we had trusted you. I was young, in love, and ignorant, too. But what kind of lowlife does that?"

"I know, Edna. I can't apologize. It's not in me to say I was wrong."

For a minute, Edna seemed to soften. "Why did you take that woman with you?" She waited.

"If it's any comfort, she left me in St. Louis and took half of the money," he answered.

That snapped Edna back. "I wish I could pity you, Freddie, but I can't. Your heart must have shriveled and died a long time ago."

For a moment, I wondered if he was going to beg for forgiveness. Surely not Freddie Garcia. He was pure evil, coated in arrogance.

She stopped and took a deep breath. "It's too late to spare you. You will find a way to keep taking what isn't yours, shaping the goodness of others into a salve of doubting applied to our wounds.

"And did you kill Preacher for Guido? Because something was missing from the auction house? Preacher didn't have good sense," she said. "He didn't deserve to die, and you know it."

She snatched the long, sharp letter opener from her desk and pointed it at Rico.

"One more chance? One more forgiving heart? No way, Freddie. I have had enough, and so has this town. In some ways, you are worse than Mr. S. You knew us long ago. Walked our streets, slept in our beds, knew our people, and left. There's no welcome back into our arms. I am tired and weakened by this."

Her words hung there in the silence. Edna's shoulders slumped, and she closed her eyes. I held my breath hidden in the dark. Then a flush rushed up her neck. She opened her eyes. They blazed like a righteous bolt of lightning thrown out of the very hand of Madam.

She spat out the words clearly with a waspish bite. "What am I gonna do with you, Freddie? I want to kill you, but what would happen to me?" She twirled the silver letter opener between her fingers.

"What is a fate worse than death for Freddie Garcia?"

"Living without you, Edna."

He stepped in front of her as if to touch her, but he didn't. There was silence. I couldn't see Edna. Freddie stood there blocking her from my sight. Then Edna walked around the desk and stood beside Freddie. Looking into his face, she said, "Meshac, come here."

I emerged from the porch and came to her side. Freddie stared at me and folded his arms.

"We have the Bugatti. But to get it back, you've got to stand before Nuanz and tell them the truth."

Freddie said nothing; in fact, he was weaving a bit.

"There's a meeting on court square tonight at eight o'clock. People have been taking sides and spreading rumors. We need to turn this around now. You'll have a chance to make it right. We will return the Bugatti with the understanding that you and Salvatorre leave Nuanz."

"But what do you expect me to say?"

"I don't care. Just make it sound good for now and then quietly fade away into the night. You and Guido."

He nodded his head. Edna sighed and told me, "I need a moment alone with Rico. Wait for me in the car, and I'll drive you down when I finish here."

39

Gathering on the Square

Accusations had been flying all week since the Oasis burned, and Deacon was nowhere to be found. Then last night, the Confederate soldier statue on the court square fell over. His head rolled down the wide sidewalk and stopped at the bottom of the stairs leading into the courthouse. No one saw who was responsible. There were names called and people blamed who had no plausible connection at all. People were suspicious and pointing fingers at their fellow citizens. Word spread quickly that the mayor had called a town meeting at the courthouse this evening. That gave Edna a ready-made audience to take her stand.

When we arrived at twilight, a good-sized crowd had gathered at the front portico. Yellow crime tape roped off the area. Everyone had their backs turned to the decapitated statue. The sky was dusky, waiting with a couple of stars. Soon the moon would rise over the east side of the square. The courthouse clock face glowed.

Noc Taliafarro climbed the steps and raised his arms over his head. Quietness descended on the murmuring crowd. The light from the hallway shone through the open courthouse doors and backlit Noc. He looked even taller and more imposing there, especially since grim, white faces surrounded him. The black citizens formed a semicircle around the south entrance. They stood shoulder to shoulder. Some had their children standing in front of them; others were solitary. But there was no daylight between those black bodies.

In the quiet, Noc's voice was as deep and melodious as a bass guitar.

"We are here to solve some problems. No one wants to hurt anyone or be hurt. We are all looking for the truth."

He paused, and a car squealed its tires as it took off down College Street. Those in the back turned, but the tight circle of black folks kept their heads turned toward Noc.

"We have had quite a summer, and we know something ain't right here in our town. We are trusting that the police will find the real culprit and make him pay." He paused as a few shifted on their feet and nodded their heads.

"Nobody is trying to escape punishment. We seek justice."

Then he paused for a moment, and when he did, a big, white owl swooped down from the oak tree and whooshed by us with a hollow, deep hoot. We jumped.

"A little skittish, are you?" Noc shook his head. We laughed—all of us. Then we waited.

"But we want to be heard. That's all. So listen. Think."

At that point, the circle of black people stepped forward in unison. Somehow, the white people began forming a second half circle behind them. Miss Lewis, Mary Craig, Mrs. Buford, and the schoolteacher, Miss Annie, nudged the white women closer. They never looked back to see how many followed them but only looked straight ahead. They stood like a hedge of protection. Grace and I joined the others. We locked arms and stood.

As the mood changed, Sheriff Hensley asked the crowd, "Is Edna Love here?"

She had let me out before she drove the Caddy to the north side of the square. Suddenly, we felt the crowd divide and move as Edna made her way through the concentric circles and up the steps. The men and Edna talked for a moment and then went inside. People moved restlessly. All eyes were glued on the doors. The sheriff and Noc emerged. Noc stepped forward.

"Edna Love has something she needs to say to us. She will introduce you to a person who can tell us all the truth. Give us just a few more minutes."

He went back inside. We could see people standing there in the hallway behind the glass doors. The crowd grew larger, but the voices were still quiet. Soon they would be restless if someone didn't do something. I scanned the crowd for Rico, but I didn't see him anywhere. Then Noc, Edna, the sheriff, and the mayor came out on the porch. Noc indicated that Edna should speak.

Placing one hand on her hip with those chopsticks glittering in the dim light, Edna leaned on Noc's folded arm. She said to the crowd, "Everyone, I know we've all been through some hard times these last few months. But things are coming to light at last. Give us a few more minutes."

Edna leaned over and said something to Noc. They went back inside.

We stood there, not knowing what exactly to do.

Suddenly, people moved and talked to each other; kids darted across the square and the talk hit a normal level. I could hear bits and pieces of conversations. Some said they had to get home. The kids needed to be in bed. Some of the parents walked away, calling to their kids. I wondered what had happened to Rico.

Edna and the Clock Tower

Was there going to be any kind of announcement? Maybe not. I wondered if Rico had skipped out on Edna and if the sheriff knew what she had planned. People shook their heads and grumbled, and the black folks got ready to head back home. Some kids had snatched the crime tape and ran around with it trailing behind them. Most of us were still mesmerized by the fallen Confederate soldier. His head lay there in the grass. The body precariously leaned on its side. Who could have done that and why?

Then a gunshot, followed by a deep, hollow strike of the clock, caused us to look up. Edna Love stood there in the clock tower, the light falling around her like a white robe. She held a gun high over her head, pointing straight up to the sky. She stirred some of us from a deep trance into quivering at the sight. Then she pulled the trigger again—*ding, ding, ding.*

We took a collective breath. Our precious bell from the first courthouse. The one that later survived the fire in 1941. The bell that rang only when the spirit moved it. The sound that could travel on a quiet Saturday afternoon in summer all the way out of the West Levee to the setting sun. We waited for whatever the inevitable follow-up would be. No one moved. No one said a word. Then Edna lowered the gun and placed her hand on the white column there.

Her voice was strong and sure:

"I made a grave mistake, my friends. One that is not possible to ever recover from, I believe. I ..." She shook her head. " I ..." She took a step closer to the railing as if she wanted to see us better. But it scared us, seeing her that close to the edge.

As if we were one person, we stepped closer, wanting to keep her there, strong and straight.

Look at us, I thought. *Look at how we feel about you, Edna Love. It's written here on everyone's face. Look at us, Edna.* I wanted to shout it, but she was too far away. She couldn't feel us.

Suddenly, there was a bright light in the sky, drawn down to focus on Edna. The theater searchlight, still on the bank roof from the Christmas ticket drawing, spotlighted her.

As we quieted, she said, "I have done something that is unforgivable. You may think there's nothing that can't be forgiven, but there is. If you can't make things right, then nothing but misery lies ahead."

We strained to hear her voice. The light began its rotation around the square. She didn't seem to notice, and her next words were spoken in the semidarkness.

"I used to think most everybody deserves a second chance. I kept wanting to believe that—but I just don't know. I kept making mistakes even when I knew better."

A hush fell over us as we huddled on the front lawn. We were frozen in place.

"Here in Nuanz, we care about each other. I thought we did. That's why we're here.

"We care when a little child is drowned and beaten and thrown in a pool. We care when an old woman bathes in the community fountain. We watch the town dog or Henry Malone guard our courthouse, and we wonder and wait. But when we do nothing, our hearts become stones. Then we lose."

Even the children were quiet, waiting for the circle of light to come back around to the clock tower.

"Listen to me, Nuanz. I have led you to the jumping-off place. I didn't mean to. You trusted me, and I thought I knew it all."

Edna stopped then and leaned over, trying to be closer to us. "But I know this much. When I know I am wrong, I have to do what's right. When guilt and shame bend you, it's hard to stand up straight, but here I am."

She stood there for a moment as the light made its slow, circular motion around the square. Its brilliance hit the top of the oak trees, sending a blue funnel of light into the black sky. Next, the beacon illuminated the red slate roof tiles all the way to the thin pinnacle of the clock tower pointing to God himself. The spotlight stayed there a moment, then skimmed down the other side and silently began its slow circle around the square. The feed store sign glistened in the white light that bounced on the street, glanced over the five-and-dime windows, jaggedly bounced toward the stars above College Street, and crawled to the west side over the Bluebird Cafe front. The arc took around half a minute but seemed longer until Edna was illuminated again in the spotlight. Her words had an edge that pricked our hearts as we waited there in the darkness.

"I had to end this since I started it. The losses keep piling up. Preacher is dead. Deacon got beaten up and ran away. And now Freddie Garcia, who is also known as Rico Martes, is missing. Johnny lies in the back of an ambulance on his way to the hospital."

She took another breath. "The Oasis is burned down. Mr. S is still out there somewhere. We all thought he brought us prosperity. He didn't. He brought criminals to Nuanz. I take the responsibility. I fell for his act, and I led you to believe it, too. I take the blame."

We stood there in our grief and our shock. No one knew what to do next. Just as the light began its next movement, we saw a man standing behind Edna. We shouted, "Look, Edna! Behind you."

She paid us no attention. Then the light began its arc. I turned to Queen. "That's gotta be Rico. We need to get up there now."

We began shouting, "Edna, Edna, look out! Look behind you!"

All we could make out was the tall figure of a man, his shadow long and forbidding. He reached around her and pulled her back to the floor. We began to move on the ground. Somebody shouted, "Get the sheriff! Quick! Run up there now!"

There was confusion at first, and the crowd ran toward the steps to enter the building.

"Wait!" the mayor shouted. "Wait for the sheriff!"

Someone else yelled, "We can't wait. Let's go. Now. Move."

Voices were frantic and frightened. A woman shouted from the back of the crowd. "Look! He's hurting her!"

She pointed toward the tower. We started back down the steps, wanting to see what was going on in the tower.

The sheriff sent a deputy to lock the doors. Others began running up the stairs. Several men shook the locked doors, trying to get in.

"Quick." I tugged on Queen's arm. "Take us through the basement."

We jumped off the porch side and went in the basement door. The janitor watched us run inside, and Queen grabbed his arm. "Uncle, we got to get up to the tower now. What's the fastest way?"

He shook his head. "The freight elevator went up a while ago. I heard it creaking. It ain't come back down."

"We got to get up there. They got the other doors locked."

"You'll have to climb up the stairs through the attic, I reckon."

"Please. Somebody's gonna get hurt!"

He fumbled for his keys and pulled one out. We followed him through a cubbyhole, past the mops and brooms. He held the curtain back on the wall as we passed through. In the dark, he pointed toward a wall.

"There, behind those boxes."

We cleared away the boxes, and he unlocked the door. An old, wooden staircase was boxed off in a tiny room, winding around itself.

"This takes you to the attic. From there, you'll have to go to the far wall and up the ladder there and open the trapdoor to the tower."

We took the steps quietly to the attic. There were piles of ledgers, boxes stacked against the wall, and odds and ends scattered everywhere. Broken chairs and discarded tables were all over the room.

We found the door to the tower. Inside was another set of stairs, dark and narrow, but somehow, I led the way. Queen was behind me, whispering, "Go. Go faster, Mesha."

The stairs were so steep and close that I could reach with my hands and feel the next step as I tried to climb faster. Spiderwebs and dust flew everywhere. We climbed. I couldn't hear the crowd any longer, just me and Queen and our labored breathing in the steep, dark passageway. I imagined Edna trying to get away, but where could she go? We climbed steadily from the attic floor. My heart pounded against my ribcage. There was no time to think, only move.

Queen and I struggled with the trapdoor, trying to push it open. Just as we felt it give way, we heard the gun go off. I raised the trapdoor enough to see out. Edna stood there with her gun laid across her chest. Then she fired another warning shot, which ricocheted off the bell and knocked a hole in the clock. We heard the tinkle of broken glass, and the bell reverberated. We crouched down on the stairs, holding the trapdoor balanced on my head.

There was a narrow crack, but we saw Edna's high heels and heard a man's voice. As Rico lunged for her, we pushed the hatch wider. I saw her level the gun straight at his heart. He backed away. Edna kept on, step by step. We stayed there, not daring to breathe or speak. He backed away until he felt the railing behind him. She kept coming. He slid one leg over the side and tried to gain a footing on the slick tiles.

Edna spoke. "Freddie. You shouldn't have ever come back. You fool. Now I've got to kill you, and what will happen to me then?"

He closed his eyes and shrugged his shoulders. She backed away a step. Her back was to us, and I could barely make out her words.

"I thought it might. I thought . . ." She lowered the gun.

Queen placed her hand on the last rung and shoved me with her shoulder.

She whispered in my ear. "Come on. We gotta go. Push, push up now."

I crept out on my hands and knees, staying as low as I could while Queen held the top. I looked around for something to throw or protect us with, but there was only a coiled rope on top of a pile of canvas. Queen held a hammer and handed me something. All I knew was that it felt heavy.

Then Rico reached over and grabbed Edna's wrist with one hand and closed his other hand over the barrel. He held it high over his head. He pulled her back to the railing. He still had one leg over the railing and one on the roof tiles. He gripped her wrist tight, and the gun dangled in his other hand. She reached back with her other hand, trying to steady herself or pull away from him.

"Edna, I wish it could have been different."

Her back was to me, but I heard her words. "So do I."

She glanced back at me. Then she said, "Always . . . close."

She bowed her head. I peered around the bell then as Rico loosened his grasp on her. The gun in his other hand was lowered beside him. They both stood there looking at each other, their hands entwined. Then Rico's eyes rolled back. He shook his head. His face was gray. The spotlight began its sweep again. We were still crouched behind the bell.

I stood and shouted, "Let her go!"

Rico startled. He raised the gun. The searchlight reflected off the bell into his eyes, and he blinked. Then he must have shifted his weight or tried to bring the other leg over the railing. Suddenly, a red balloon of blood appeared on his face and poured down his neck. He reached with one hand to pull the chopstick from his cheek. He windmilled his arms. I heard the gun clatter over the roof tiles. Then Rico disappeared down the back eaves of the courthouse.

Edna crumpled to the floor with her back to the railing. It all happened so fast. I ran over to her. Queen said, "Give her some room."

We huddled beside her in the darkness. Clouds shifted over the moon. The night swallowed it all. Even the voices faded away. The sheriff should be here any minute now. Ole Davy Crockett below us saw nothing at all. He still faced east, staring over his shoulder. The searchlight returned its sweep. But darkness hovered over our beloved Nuanz.

Queen and I led Edna down the steps to the attic room. The sheriff was there with his deputy holding the freight elevator door. No one spoke, and we huddled together as the motor moved the huge pulley and started our descent. Edna's face crumpled, and her hair straggled down one side. She dropped something into my hand. I said nothing. The rumble stopped, and the deputy slid the door open.

The cool breeze welcomed us, and we stepped onto the courthouse back lawn. Mr. Gordon and Lawyer Malone stood with their arms folded across their chests. They stepped forward to help us get through the crowd. I held Edna's arm and kept moving.

Two of the sheriff's deputies, including the one called Tyler, ran up to the sheriff. I heard Tyler say, "No sign of Rico back there. Saw some crushed vines pulled off the wall and blood on them. He could have held onto them maybe. There was lots of footprints. Mitchell's looking for Rico's car."

Sheriff Hensley nodded. "Keep looking."

He turned to the crowd. "Everything's okay now. Y'all need to go on home. We've got this under control."

Some began moving; others kept staring. Queen looked at me, nodded her head, and disappeared. I scanned the crowd for Noc or Madam, but they did not appear. Lawyer Malone took Edna's other arm then and said, "We need to get you checked out, Edna. Are you okay?"

She didn't speak. I said, "I'll go with you."

The sheriff agreed with us, and the crowd made a path. We found our way over to Lawyer Malone's office. During the long night, Sheriff Hensley determined that Edna Love had acted in self-defense and that Rico Martes/Freddie Garcia had lost his balance and had fallen off the roof onto the ground below. She'd had a gun, yes, but she didn't shoot Rico with it. Nobody knew where Rico was. Sheriff Hensley took Edna home. Her Cadillac was the only car left on the square now.

As I made my way back to my apartment, Noc Taliafarro stepped out of the shadows. I expected him. There were only the two of us now. I waited for him to speak.

I thought it must be close to dawn, but the sky was still black, studded with a brilliance of stars.

When Noc stopped at the bench there to light his pipe, I joined him. He took a few draws, then shook the flame away. He broke the match with his thumb and tucked it into his shirt pocket.

"What a night." His pipe glowed and the smoke floated out of his mouth with his words. "Is Miss Edna all right?"

"Yes. The sheriff and Lawyer Malone decided Edna was not to blame."

"Hmm," he said.

"The gun was empty where they found it wedged in the shrubbery behind the courthouse. She never shot him, you know. I was there. She shot everything else but him. Poor old clock."

We both looked up at the dark clock tower. Noc nodded and tilted his head back to look at the stars. I did the same.

"But seems like Rico walked or crawled away. There's no body to be found," I said, still gazing at the stars, and then I studied Noc's face.

"What happened, Noc?"

He crossed his long legs and leaned back against the bench. His hands were big, and the lit pipe seemed to float up to his face.

"Well, I told you I'd do my part. I promised Edna."

I waited.

"Edna and me had a plan if Rico didn't go along. When he didn't show on the front porch there, I knew we would have to move to our next plan."

He looked straight ahead and shook his head a bit.

"Which was what?"

"If he didn't show, then Edna would try and lure him to the clock tower. If she made it there, no one could stop her from speaking the truth that had to be said. Maybe this would work—we didn't know for sure. But he must have been watching, trying to grab her."

Noc's voice was steady and quiet. "When Rico disappeared from the tower, we were ready on the back side.

"Boy Blue, Rem, and Sun Man were stationed around the back, ready. He was in a daze still when he rolled down the last twenty feet. The ivy always clings to the incinerator shaft there, and a man can grab hold and slow down his fall. But he hit his head on that crumbling brick flower box back there. The vines mostly covered it. He laid there in a heap, and

Rem had him picked up and in Rico's car before anybody even noticed. He was dead before he hit the ground. Rem drove off in the car. We stayed there until you and Edna walked out with the sheriff.

"Evil catches up to you. It caught up to him. As it is, Miss Edna can't be blamed because he fell. I think the moonflowers set him back some, but that final fall down the roof got him."

"And?"

"Well, we don't want nobody like Salvatorre going after Miss Edna."

Noc looked at me then. "You know Rico—Freddie . . ." Noc shrugged his shoulders. "Blood was on his hands. Nuanz blood. We got enough to handle here without outsiders interfering, stirring up people. Blaming others when they are the culprits."

"We took his car out toward Lovers Lane. That back road leading off Paradise Alley."

"Yes. I remember it."

"The swamp gases was working. It's pretty eerie out there with those green lights."

"I know very well."

He turned to me then.

"Where is he?"

Noc looked at me before he answered. His words were slow and measured.

"We took him and his car on to the edge of the swamp there past Paradise Alley down Christmasville Road. The little north fork of the river—she winds her way up from the river bottom west of town to the red clay on the east side of town."

Noc took another pull on his pipe and then looked at me.

"You know, the river is full of water moccasins here in August. They've bedded down low where it's cooler. And there's plenty of fish." I shuddered at the very thought.

"We took his license plate and papers and set him behind the wheel and then pushed him down that little incline into the water."

The quietness seemed to grow on us then. As if there was no sense in pursuing this any further.

"So was he dead or not? I gotta know."

Noc drew the last pull out of his pipe and turned to me.

"Mesha, the world is full of good and evil. No matter what we may try to do. Sometimes you can let things run their own course. Other times, you have to step in and push a bit. The moonflowers pushed. The evil got him."

He looked at me then. "You and Miss Edna don't have to worry about Rico ever again."

I felt a lightness in me then like the moonlight that played over the dark courthouse, the tall oak trees, the fountain that washed away more than the Whittakers' sins, and the noble statue of Davy Crockett. Suddenly, Henry Malone nudged me on my arm as Noc disappeared into the darkness toward Paradise Alley.

Strangers come and go here in Nuanz. Some stay; some return; some disappear.

Henry sat beside me, waiting for the scratch on his head. The past rose up as it always does. Justification comes in waves. Noc led the way last night in the darkness as his ancestors had. To do the hard work takes somebody who's stronger than most of us. The hard work is not always pretty, but it has to be done.

I was alone at last, gazing out my bedroom window at downtown Nuanz. I dug out the Crown Royal bag, and the tiger was resting on my table.

Deacon never heard of Rembrandt Bugatti. He surely didn't know what art was, but he felt it. He felt the strength of the tiger in that lump of clay, which became a living, breathing thing to him. Deacon felt the tiger's heart beating for him. Protecting him and his world. So did I. I was not letting go, either.

I thought I may keep the tiger. Mr. Guido Salvatorre be damned. Hell, I didn't know. I shouldn't even have it. What should I do now?

I could stand the tiger on top of the cigarette machine in the Bluebird Cafe, directly underneath the board with today's menu. Or maybe inside the glass candy counter between the Moon Pies and Jawbreakers. Burning brightly—his tail in mid-swish—waiting to pounce.

Gently, I wrapped my tiger in the Crown Royal bag and put it in a box, hidden in a corner of my kitchen shelf.

Madam's moonflower vines snaked all over Paradise Alley. They knew the best place to survive. The fragrant white flowers never open until darkness falls. The dark brings them to life.

A few could be spotted in other places, like the rainspout in the alley by Mr. Harwood's office. A tiny one inched its way up the charred post by the Oasis. A bank of them grew in the darkness under the platform of the train depot. But the biggest show of moonflowers was still Paradise Alley. If only the feel of Paradise Alley could wind its way through our little town like the moonflowers. There's a feeling of protection there that springs from the darkness. Those hidden places that offer acceptance and refuge. In Paradise Alley, you can find good and evil, courage and fear, strength and weakness. They exist side by side. After all, we cannot have one without the other.

Maybe we could sweeten the air with that magic, like Madam's moonflowers. It would float into our bedrooms, underneath the basement windows, down forgotten chimneys, and over the courthouse tower like a layer of moon dust. Perhaps then, we might see things differently. We might learn to balance our lives the best we can, wherever our Paradise Alley may be. Who knows?

Strangers come and go; some stay, but others leave and never come back. But this we do know: We all need a connection. Everyone needs a reason to get up every day. A place that feels comfortable. For some, maybe the Bluebird offers that comfort. When you look up at the courthouse clock, when a kid takes hold of your hand, or when Henry Malone guards the town. We must remember we are in this together.

Madam's moonflowers had faded. We were waiting for the oak trees to change color in the court square. The Whittakers had stayed out of the fountain since the first frost fell. It was near freezing now. The Confederate soldier was restored to his perch. Davy Crockett's words still shone in the moonlight: "Be sure you're right, then go ahead."

Henry Malone came and sat beside me like he always does when I take a break outside the Bluebird. I claimed the bench as ours, and when he laid his nose in my lap, I lifted his ears and whispered secrets. I stroked his back, and his eyes told me his secrets. I unwrapped some bacon for him that he crunched before he lay down, belly full, and snored in the sunshine.

And Joe? He got another job down in New Orleans that paid more. He showed up as usual after his long months away on the river, and we walked up to my apartment after I got off work. I packed a plate of hoop cheese and saltine crackers to go with us, but I was unprepared for what came next.

After I set up our snack on my table, he held me in his arms, kissed my neck, and said, "I love you. Come with me, Meshac. I've got a good job offer in New Orleans that pays more working for a big ship company. I'll take good care of you."

I was shocked, but I had figured something was going on. He seemed restless when he was here in Nuanz with me.

"And how long will you be gone on those sea cruises?" I asked, bending my head back to look into his gray eyes. He meant it, I knew. But he'd be gone even longer.

He looked at me and nodded his head. "I got no ties in Nuanz but you, Mesha. It's time, you know. We need to do some living."

I was scared, but I knew what my answer was. I had a lump in my throat as big as a river rock. "Joe, I have to work. I can't lay around all day like some high-falutin' kept woman."

He smiled. "But you know I gotta do this, don't you? It's a good chance for me."

"Yes, and I am still figuring things out for me."

Maybe we could have lasted. But I wasn't sure I was ready to give up Edna, Grace, Queen, Mr. Rob, and Henry. When Joe left for good, Henry was waiting for me at the bottom of my apartment steps. I swear, that brown-eared dog knows everything. We sat on the steps, and I cried into his fur.

I miss Joe. Maybe he'll come back someday. We had lit a tiny candle of light and hope and a little love once. I may regret letting him go without me. But this little town makes me feel safe—different than any other place I've been. I even think they like me. I can't leave that, at least not now.

Edna just said, "Mesha, love comes and goes, and it will come around again." And we drank gin fizzes on the building roof.

Edna got her insurance money to rebuild the Oasis, and that was giving the construction folks, carpenters, and painters plenty to do. She promised it was "gonna be grand, Mesha" while her chopsticks glittered in the sunshine.

Mr. Salvatorre and Lydia returned one night to Nuanz. No one saw them but Noc Taliafarro, who was out on one of his nightly walks. They packed their car and never acknowledged him at all. He told Edna and the sheriff, though. The auction house is locked now, and the moving vans came and emptied most of the house.

Everything stayed put in the gallery, until one bright fall day, when I love to see the maples turn yellow and red, the FBI came from Washington. There were about five agents, looking spiffy in their suits. They cut the padlock off the auction house and went right in with movers, who brought their trucks and carried everything back to DC.

That was the big talk in the Bluebird. The ladies of the Literary Club and the old men of the Liars' Table 'bout fell off their chairs gossiping. I served the FBI agents when they ate at the cafe. They were polite, tipped well, and left everybody alone. They learned our specials in a snap, and they even ate our big cheeseburgers and French fries. Not like some of those female antique hunters from months ago who only wanted a salad with oil and vinegar, then complained because we didn't ice our lettuce to make it crisp. Who's got time to do that?

If the FBI agents had talked about the auction house, I'd have listened as hard as I could without my ears falling off, but they were careful. I learned more than I wanted to know about where the best fishing was in Tennessee. One day, they were at their table in the back; the next day, they were gone.

Sheriff Hensley didn't push too hard on what anyone saw or knew about that night at the courthouse clock tower. The search for Rico had stopped. But the sheriff did come to see me one September day with an inventory list in hand.

We sat at my little table in my apartment, and I hoped he didn't see my sweaty armpits. I knew my chickens had come home to roost.

"Meshac, I got a letter from Memphis the other day from a retired police officer who works at a church that serves meals to some folks down on their luck. Deacon has been there and rambled one night about Nuanz, a tiger, Mr. Salvatorre, Preacher, and you."

"The FBI has found nearly all the art and valuables Salvatorre stole. They didn't find a bronze tiger. The previous owner has offered an award for it." He paused, lifting his razor-sharp blue eyes to me. "You know anything about that tiger?"

I could have said no. But I've found my chance at redemption in Nuanz. I'm not going to let it go.

My heart thumped in my chest as I went to get the old box and the tiger in the Crown Royal bag from the back of my kitchen shelf.

"Deacon gave me this to keep for him," I said, swallowing hard as I handed over my tiger.

"And you've done a good job," Sheriff Hensley said quietly. "I'll see you get the reward."

That's all he said as he left, carrying my tiger, tiger, still burning bright in my memories.

My tiger wouldn't have looked good on the shelf under the menus at the Bluebird anyway. I told Edna that when I poured her coffee.

Down at Rem's Place, they say that Henry Malone visits Madam sometimes and they stand together at the edge of the Forked Deer River on moonlit nights. They guard something there—out past Paradise Alley. Both are vigilant while watching the moon's reflection on the dark water. Who knows? Some secrets never go away. They linger sometimes, waiting to come to light. If that is true like certain bodies, we must always remember to bury them deep.

In my dreams, I know that payback is hell. The tiger's tail swings. He paces and stalks. The moonflower blooms in the dark.

We look up at the moon that gives us tides rolling forevermore through our lives.

Edna's book of secrets—she put it in my hand that night for a reason. I kept learning about myself, and Edna kept teaching me lessons.

This is what she wrote for me in her book:

"Tell Mesha the real beauty of revenge is when you leave it behind.

Whether you exacted your revenge or you gave it over for something better. Like when you finally forgive yourself. That's when you start to live. Forgive yourself, hon."

I guess God or the angels or whatever powers there are decided I deserved a dose of hope.

Sheriff Hensley brought me the reward, $5,000, more money than I had ever seen. He helped me set up my first bank account. My hands got sweaty when I passed that check over to Mr. Wallace, the bank manager.

Mr. Rob and I made a deal. I paid him $1,000 as my start on buying the Bluebird. It'll likely take me twenty years to pay. He said that makes me a real part owner in the Bluebird, well, not a big part, but a part.

I'm still not giving him free apple pie, though.

Every now and then, someone at the Liars' Table munches on their cornbread and wonders out loud what happened to Rico. But not around Edna Love.

41

Epilogue

So the Bugatti cat is gone from Nuanz. I still think of its sleek, coiled body there crouching on my table, plus that poem that wagged its tail over us all those weeks. "Burning bright in the forests of the night."

Tonight, I am gazing at the moon again. Her reflected light is empowered by our watchful eyes. The moon drinks light from the now-vanished sun.

Millions of us watch and wait. We depend on her to be there and hold us safe here on earth. We watch and wait and hope.

I want to say to those watchers—burn bright like the moon. To Gracie and Deacon. Queen and Florence. Even Joe and Madam. Burn bright like the fires that frightened the wampus cat. Or the flames that began the resurrection of Edna and rebuilt the Oasis. Burn till you shine. Burn till all that is left is durable, unbending mettle. Like me. That's what I am shooting for. Burn bright.

About the Author

"Writing and yoga are a natural link between the physical ordinary world and the inner work needed to explore and understand ourselves. Stories must be told to help us sift through life and to endure. Practicing yoga and paying attention remain the two vital parts of my writing life. I don't know where I would be without them."

Nancy Hall and her husband renovated a grain bin known as the Diva Den, where she writes, teaches yoga, and watches sunsets.

Burn Bright is Nancy's second Southern mystery novel in the Tilted series. *Tilted*, her debut novel, received five-star reviews.

www.ingramcontent.com/pod-product-compliance
Lightning Source LLC
Chambersburg PA
CBHW041053310726
48978CB00011BA/536